Dreamside

GRAHAM JOYCE
Dreamside

A Tom Doherty Associates Book
New York

DREAMSIDE

This book is printed on acid-free paper.

First published in 1991 by Pan Books Ltd., London, UK

A Tor Book
Published by Tom Doherty Associates, LLC
175 Fifth Avenue
New York, NY 10010

www.tor.com

Tor® is a registered trademark of Tom Doherty Associates, LLC.

Library of Congress Cataloging-in-Publication Data

Joyce, Graham.
    Dreamside / Graham Joyce.
       p.   cm.
    "A Tom Doherty Associates book."
    ISBN 0-312-86633-X (hc)
    ISBN 0-312-87546-0 (pbk)
    1. Dreams—Fiction.   I. Title.
PR6060.O93 D74   2000
823'.914—dc21   00-027714

First Tor Hardcover Edition: June 2000
First Tor Trade Paperback Edition: March 2001

Printed in the United States of America

0 9 8 7 6 5 4 3 2 1

TO SUZANNE
THERE WHEN THE DREAMING STARTED

Dreamside

PROLOGUE

Behold, this dreamer cometh
—Genesis

Lee was having trouble sleeping. It was already near dawn, and blades of light were slipping between the ribs of the blind. He'd spent the night on the edge of sleep, but every time he let go, something stirred in the dark and shook him awake. Not scary exactly, but enough of a jolt to flip him out of sleep. He opened his eyes. It was easier to give up.

The luminous dial on his clock blinked: outside a horn blared. He felt sticky and sweaty. His bed was a knot of sheets, his eyes were pasted half shut, and his hair stood up in a quiff. Fumbling to the bathroom, he turned on the shower and scalded himself.

It had been a strange night. A dervish of unfathomable, fevered images had crowded his dreams. Now they were sluicing away, as though painted on his skin. He threw on his once white towelling robe and went into his kitchen. Somewhere a time-set radio switched itself on and a breakfast voice piped feebly. He took an egg and cracked it on a pan but it didn't break. He tried a second time. Again it didn't break. "Oh, no," he said, "oh, no . . ." Raising the egg close to his face, he blew on it sharply.

Then he woke up.

Daylight streaming in through the blinds picked out needles of perspiration on his face. The luminous clock dial winked at him. A horn blared outside, someone with their hand pressed down hard. He sat up, bedclothes slithering to a heap on the floor, and staggered to the bathroom. The shower made him catch his breath, gooseflesh popping as he walked into the icy pyramid of rushing water. This time he had a clear impression of what he had been dreaming the moment before he woke up.

In his kitchen, the time-set radio switched itself on. His eggs frying in the pan looked back at him with cartoon eyes, and he lost his appetite. He got dressed for work and pulled on his overcoat.

Outside, the earth was in the grip of its own dream, February frost that sucked the sound out of everything. He broke its spell with billows of exhaust that had the frost imps hacking and coughing and running for cover. *Awake awake awake*; that was what his wipers said. *Awake awake awake*. Slipping the clutch he put the car into gear.

And woke up.

The clock blinked. A horn blared. He was afraid to turn on the shower in case he should wake up back in bed. He looked in the mirror. A frightened face looked back at him.

His nerves were torn and he had a bad taste in his mouth. In the kitchen a radio switched itself on, and something fell away inside him. He turned, looked at the radio, then at the plug. He disconnected the plug from the socket and the radio died. He reconnected the plug and the voice picked up where it had left off.

He got into his car and sat behind the wheel in silence for a moment. Lee was the habitual early bird, always driving to work with his radio turned up loud, always first there. He turned into the empty car park behind the advertising agency and parked.

And woke up.

He lay in the dark of his room, panting, pressing himself into his mattress. The clock dial winked mutinously. The horn of a car sounded outside, falling away into the distance. This could go on for ever, he told himself. He wished he could tunnel out of it by going back to sleep, but he knew it was futile to try. There was no choice.

So he did it all again. Shower; oh no. Radio; not that. Breakfast; please God. Knowing all of the time that this could, and maybe would, go on for ever.

Dreaming. Would he ever wake up?

He needed something to convince him that he was awake, really awake. He brushed the back of his hand across the flame. He felt the hairs on his wrist begin to singe and got an unmistakable whiff of burned hair. It was a wide-awake smell.

Outside was the same frost-crisp morning. The car coughed into life. He drove to his office with excessive caution, and parked in a different place. The three flights of stairs left him short-winded, and he was breathing hard when he heard his phone ringing. Hurrying down the corridor, he pushed open the office door and reached across his desk to take the call. As he stretched, the expanse of desk seemed to grow and the telephone retreated from his fingers. He was unable to reach it, and, with each ring, the signal prickled with renewed urgency.

He woke up with his bedside phone ringing. It had the clarity of sound of a razor sawing on bone. He jackknifed awake and reflex-caught the receiver.

"Lee?" A woman's voice. "Lee Peterson? Is that you?"

PART ONE

February 1986

O N E

I had a dream, which was not all a dream
—Byron

There was no forgetting her voice. After more than twelve years, it was Ella Innes.

"Ella! Oh, Ella! I know why you've called me. It's happening isn't it, it's all happening again!"

"Hold on Lee; it'll be OK. Listen, we've really got to talk."

"Yes. Only it's not OK Ella. I don't know if I'm awake or if I'm dreaming; or if we're even having this conversation."

"You're awake now. This is real. Remember how I used to wake you? This is just the same, remember."

Remember. It was a kind of code word. Remember. I remember it all. Your voice. Your strange scent. How I felt every time you came near me.

"Sure." But he sounded more than doubtful. "Let me just get my thoughts together will you? It's been a wicked night."

"I had to get in touch with you. I couldn't think of anything else." He heard her take a deep breath. "I want to come and see you. Today."

"Today? Why today? Where the hell are you anyway?" (Who the hell are you after all this time?)

"I'm living in Cumbria, by the sea. Nice scenery and nuclear seepage. What else do you want to know?"

"But that's over two hundred and fifty miles away, Ella."

"We live in a world of cars and motorways, Lee. It's incredible how easy it is to travel around."

"OK, no need to be funny with me." But that was Ella. He thought for a moment before giving her some muddled directions. "All right. I'll be here waiting for you."

"Do it." That's how she always used to talk. Just do it.

"One thing before you go, Ella. How did you track me down? I mean it's been a long time."

"Not so difficult. I started at the university and followed a very orthodox career trail." Old note of criticism, not fair. "Lee? Are you afraid?"

"I had a terrible night, Ella. Yes, I am afraid."

He put down the phone. It had been twelve going on thirteen years since they had seen or spoken to each other. He stared at the wall, dumbly. His astonishment and dismay conflicted with the acute fear of waking up and finding himself back in bed, which he knew would stay with him all day.

Then he remembered the trick with the book. Still towelling his hair dry he took, at random, a paperback volume from the bookshelf. Letting it fall open naturally, he read the first few lines to present themselves:

> *But his dominion that exceeds in this*
> *Stretcheth as far as doth the mind of man:*
> *A sound magician is a demi-god.*

Glancing away, he squeezed his eyes shut, then looked back at the open page. He was relieved to see that the lines were unchanged. He repeated the exercise. Hoping that it counted for something, he returned the book to the shelf.

When he checked back down the sequence of false awakenings, the most bizarre thing had been Ella's voice striking out of the past and talking to him as if they had spoken only yesterday. When they had parted in their youth it had not been on bad terms, or at least where there had been pain there had been no anger. Parting had happened by inevitable unspoken contract, for the simple reason that they had come to hold each other's company in a mutual despair which outweighed even their terror.

Lee inspected his face in the mirror and awarded himself a high slob rating. That man in the mirror, with the lantern jaw and the pouting bottom lip which girls had once found endearing, was now getting jowls. He could do with losing a few pounds, too. Would Ella be able to see the winsome, athletic, wise-alec twenty-year-old that he had once been?

It didn't occur to him that Ella herself would have aged. It wasn't as though he hadn't thought of her in the decade since she had fled the university, putting two thousand miles and an even greater psychic geography between them; but in his mind she had remained always the same. Unforgettable Ella; delicious, hypnotic, superior, erotic Ella; Ella undressed, Ella with her clothes on. There came, in equal measure, deep tormenting sentimental memories and sharp sexual reminiscences. This was the cocktail of nostalgia he took out and sipped from time to time, and in it, bright and sparkling, was Ella Innes, vibrant with arch cleverness and smoldering undergraduate sexuality.

Memories clung to him like the tentacles of a deep-sea creature; or perhaps that was him, sucking at memories that should have drifted free long ago. But the problem was his. All relationships post-Ella had been held up to her light by way of comparison, and inevitably in those dazzling rays they palled. Scratch the surface of Lee's feelings for any woman and you would find Ella, impossible to erase or surpass. What could others hope to do, when she ghosted the shores of his memory and seeded his dreams like that?

The only consolation to Lee, if consolation he was looking for, was that he knew that Ella could never get over him. They could live neither with nor without each other.

And now she had contacted him, after nearly thirteen years. He was going to meet her, and he was afraid, just as he knew she too would be afraid.

Ella Innes. Why did you have to come back?

TWO

To dream of holding eggs symbolizes vexation
—Astrampsychus, AD 350

Ella was late. Lee had been expecting her at around seven, and it was already after nine. He had spent two hours twitching in his armchair, jumping up from time to time to look out of the window. It had been dark for several hours and the winter sky was folded with snow.

He was physically afraid of meeting her: if she didn't show up, he wouldn't be in the least dismayed. He was already prepared to dismiss the morning's telephone call as a phantom, another dream; it would be better, far better, if the whole thing had never really happened.

Then there was a roaring underneath his window. He leaped from his seat to see headlamps blazing in his drive, clouds of exhaust in the frosty air. Lee hurried outside.

She was already climbing out of her car, an open-topped vintage sports model. She wore a flying jacket three sizes too large and a red scarf wound around her neck. She closed the door and stood motionless in the dark, looking at him.

What were they supposed to do? What was appropriate? To hug her, of course; he wanted to, but he couldn't. He couldn't even look her in the eye.

"You came down in this?" he said surveying the car. It was a fully restored spoke-wheeled 1935 MG Midget. "With the top down? In the middle of winter?"

Her breath was visible on the cold air. "It's broken. I couldn't fix it."

Lee walked around the car and began fussing with the convertible roof. "It's probably just a clip," he said.

"Lee," said Ella gently. "Leave it."

Lee looked down at his hands. He felt ridiculous. When he looked up, he saw that her eyes were fixed on his. "Of course. Let's go inside."

With the door closed behind them, Ella looked around her as if she used to own the house. When she nodded, it was as if to confirm that she found everything much as expected. Lee took her bag. "Your hands are freezing!"

Ella's smile was a reflex. "It's been a long drive."

"Maybe a drink of something?"

"Yes, something, thanks."

That was how she was; always ironic. Silver moon-and-stars earrings glimmered at her ears. They left momentary tracers in the air as she flicked her hair from her eyes. Her hastily applied lipstick looked as if it came in one piece and could be lifted off like the milk-skin from hot chocolate. Ella looked interesting rather than beautiful, and she dressed neither for the attention of men nor for the critical approval of other women. Lee was hypnotized; she was more compelling now than she had ever been as a girl of twenty.

He didn't miss a detail: her nose perhaps a couple of degrees too steep; her dark hair, long then, now worn shorter; and something like a faint cloud of suspicion in the previously startling honesty of her clear brown eyes. Underneath her flying jacket she wore a baggy pullover and slacks. She was busy unwinding the red scarf from her throat.

Her bag, a large, split-leather holdall with a broken zip, was stuffed full. Lee stowed it against an armchair. "Bohemian; you look bohemian," he said, trying to imitate her teasing manner.

Ella followed him into the kitchen, where he poured overlarge brandies and set coffee to brew. "I know I'm a mess," she said. "You look smart, that's good; and you look well." She flashed him a microsecond smile and bandaged the scarf around her hand.

"I don't know why, but I feel dull against you."

"You haven't got what it takes to be dull." In her flying jacket she looked like a wounded refugee from some fiery aerial combat. "I see you work in advertising."

"It's a job. I turn in every morning. Then I come home."

She looked at him. He felt compelled to carry on talking. "I mean it's narcotic. That's how I like it."

"You sound disappointed."

"No; I really do like it like that. But when I'm happily numb, narcotized, nodding my way through life, then *the you-know-what* starts over again."

Ella stuffed the scarf into her pocket. "That's what I'm here to talk about."

"Oh dear. Pandora wants a little chat about her box."

"Not my box; *our* box."

Lee turned towards her. "Ella, I don't want it opened up. I don't know what's going on, but it scares the liver out of me and I really don't want it opened up."

Ella put down her glass and took hold of his wrist. "Look, I don't want *it* opened up again any more than you do. I'm as frightened by it as you are. I guessed—hoped, even—that you'd be having some of the same experiences as me. I only got in touch with you because—"

Lee put his hand to her mouth. "Can we sit down?"

They moved through to the living room, Ella discarding her scarf and jacket as she went. They sat and nursed their brandies.

"I got in touch with you," Ella continued, "because of what we had together. What we did."

Silence. "I'm starving," said Ella suddenly. "What have you cooked for us?"

"Cooked? God!" He hadn't even thought about food. "I'll phone for a Chinese, shall I?"

"No food in the house, eh?" She smiled. "I couldn't help noticing the bachelor feel to the place."

"I noticed you noticing." Then Lee bit the biscuit. "Ella, will you be staying here tonight?"

"I thought I might. Unless it would be easier if I found a hotel."

"Don't be ridiculous. You'll stay here."

"Fine."

"Fine."

"Only . . . Just so that it's clear."

"So that what's clear?"

"Look; I didn't drive two hundred and fifty miles with my foot flat down on the accelerator after an absence of twelve years to start our relationship up again. I couldn't stand to have *that* opened up, as well."

"Understood," he said, waving his hands in the air, "I was just about to say that the spare room is ready for you. So you can calm down."

"I'm already calm. You don't need to tell me to calm myself."

"That's settled then."

"Right, that's settled."

Lee took this concert of understanding as a suitable moment to escape to the kitchen. He closed the door behind him, putting his back to it as he expelled a deep breath. He was furious about that business of renewing their old relationship, not with Ella but with himself. He had made his feelings transparent, trailing her with moist, spaniel eyes from the moment she had come into his house. He wanted to bury his head.

———

Their meal arrived. "Tell me," she said, "what was happening before I phoned?"

Lee glanced over his shoulder as though there might be an enemy in the room. "It started around Christmas. I thought it was just some kind of throwback. That's happened before, and there's been no problem. Since then it has come with greater frequency. Over the last few nights it has come without fail."

"Just the repeated awakening?"

"Yes. That's all, thank God; I mean there have been one or two other weird things happening in there besides, but mostly it's the repeater. It doesn't sound much but it's scaring the hell out of me."

"It's the same for me. I know how frightening it is. You get to dread every click or sudden movement in case you wake up and find yourself back in bed."

"But I've even been testing myself in the dream, burning my hand, sticking pins into myself to see if I'm in or out: it doesn't make any difference."

"That's how it was before."

"Sure, but then, somehow, even though I'd get it wrong some-times, I felt I could tell the essential difference. But not now. It gets so I don't want to bother going to work, cooking my breakfast, washing my face even, in case I wake up. Every time something just a little bit off the wall happens, or if I get a client at work with a screw loose, I end up thinking I'll wake up in five minutes and then I can go to work and deal with the real psychopaths."

"I thought *we* were the real psychopaths."

"What's worse is that the dreams make more sense than what happens when I'm awake. When I was talking to you this morning I was convinced that it was just part of another repeater and that I'd put the phone down and wake up."

"But you should have known that I'd pulled you out with the telephone. It was one of our old techniques for burrowing out. Or burrowing in."

"I know that, but I didn't ever trust it. I don't entirely trust that business with the book either."

"Can you remember anything the professor said about the repeater?"

"Only that he described it as a side effect, and said to try to enjoy it."

"Yes, he was helpful like that."

"When did it start happening with you?"

"Like you, around Christmas. Infrequently at first, then with regularity. I thought it was me; but it wasn't just repeated dreams of waking up. It was some of the other stuff."

"You went back to *that place*?" Lee was shocked.

"Not exactly. But I felt an overwhelming pull. Almost irresistible. I've been fighting it. That's why I decided I had to get in touch, find out what was happening to you."

"I know. I felt it too, pulling me back there, I mean. It was strong. I fought it. That's when the repeaters started to really take hold."

"Exactly. The more we fight off going back, the more the repeaters go to work on us."

"But what would happen if we did give in? What would happen if we really did go back there? I couldn't face it."

"At first I wondered whether you'd been there," said Ella, "whether you were up to something, trying to make contact with me."

"No."

"It was just a thought. I realize now."

"Ella, there have been many times when I've wanted you. But never like that. It didn't seem to hold so much fear for me when I was younger. Now even the thought of it can make me break into a cold sweat."

Ella ran a hand through her hair, silver moon and stars glinting at her ears. "So where does that leave us?" she asked. "If it's not you and it's not me . . . Oh God, look at us, Lee, just look at us. What a pair of casualties. I'm trying to be brave, Lee, really I am, but I'm scared. So scared."

Then Lee did what he should have done when he first saw Ella standing outside his house; he put his arms around her and kissed her, and let her cry for both of them. And when Ella cried that evening it was not only for the terror of the dreams that hung in chains around them. It was also for the unburdened, uncaring children they had been thirteen years ago, and for the thirteen years of distance and loss that had recast lovers as strangers.

"Which one of them is doing it, do you think?"

"We can't be sure that it's either of them."

An open fire burned brightly in the hearth. Ella sat close to it, her legs drawn up under her. Lee sat behind her in an armchair. "You're wrong. One of them is doing it. One of them is calling it all back. Is it him, do you think? Or is it her? We have to find out. Then we can stop them."

"I was afraid you might say that."

"No time for faint hearts," said Ella.

"You really are making a lot of assumptions. You can't know that the others are responsible for this."

"So what are your ideas?"

"Me?"

"Exactly. How long do you think it's going to be before these dreams, these repeaters turn into something else? Something more dangerous."

Lee felt like a man in a paperweight snowstorm. Everything in his life had been settled and silenced. Then Ella had arrived, had shaken the glass, and was now watching him in his blizzard.

"When push comes to shove," said Ella, "there's only one question. Is it him? Or is it her?"

"Him, her; what's the difference? It's happening."

"I think it's her. I think we'll find that she's responsible."

"Look, Ella, I'm really not convinced that we should get in touch with the others. It might not do any good. Sleeping dogs and all that. It might just make things worse. A whole lot worse. There must be something else we can do without running to them."

"We've been through this once already. It's not a question of running to them. It's a matter of not running away from them."

Lee wouldn't have minded running away from all of them, Ella included. He knew where all this was leading and he didn't like it. Ella had that manic cast to her eye. She wasn't going to be shifted.

"So what do we do?" she said.

"You're the one with all the plans."

"So it appears. Listen, it's simple. You're going to have to go after one of them; I'm going to have to go after the other. No, don't look like that. Neither of us wants to do it, but neither of us wants this thing opened up again either. You know where it can all lead, and you're just as afraid of that as I am. You also know that one of the others must be responsible for starting it up again. There can't be any other explanation. We'll have to track them down and find out what's going on."

"How the hell are we going to find them?"

"Just like I found you. We're going to use a little bit of intelligence and a little bit of insight. You'll have to take a break from selling washing powder or whatever important thing it is you do."

"I can't take time off from work! What will I tell them?"

"Tell them you're ill! Tell them you're mentally disturbed! That's something like the truth, isn't it? Our hold on reality is a little tenuous at the moment, isn't it? What do I care what you tell them?"

"Are you getting angry with me?"

"I'm just trying to give you a sense of urgency, though God knows why. This morning when I phoned you were hardly able to speak."

"I don't need reminding."

"Lee, we *could* simply do nothing about it. We *could* just forget it. Until tomorrow morning, that is, when you're going out of your mind because you don't know if you're awake or you're dreaming. Until you want to scream, and then you open your mouth and wake up. Or think you've woken up, so you want to scream again. Yes, we could do that. Then you could wonder if this conversation was all a dream."

"You can see right into my mind, can't you, Ella Innes?"

Ella softened. "Remember that psychological test the professor gave us? You're walking through the woods? You see a bear. What do you do? You always go around it. I always approach it."

"Sometimes to get a mauling."

"That's life," said Ella. "But sometimes the bear turns into a prince. You need me here, Lee. To push you on. To make you face up."

"Thanks all the same but I never had any use for a prince."

"Only for a princess, eh?"

He hated the way she reasserted her position so easily. She always seemed able to guess his thoughts. More seriously, she was already in the driving seat. He had planned not to let that happen.

He looked at her as she gazed into the grate, her skin reflecting the firelight. Yes, the years had left their mark here and there. Her face was touched with faint runes, lines of personal history he wanted to read but couldn't. As for himself, he had stopped pretending. These few hours with Ella had stripped him bare. The scaling-over of the years had been uncovered, old feelings made new, leaving him exposed, inferior, in love with her. How did she *do* that?

He leaned forward and kissed her neck. He felt her stiffen, but she didn't pull away.

"What are you doing, Lee?"

"I'm kissing you."

She turned around. "Let's not add confusion to a bad situation, eh?"

It seemed to Lee that he had been, on the contrary, trying to straighten things out. He said nothing. Ella closed the issue by standing up.

"I'm very tired. Can we say that it's settled? You go after one of them, I go after the other?"

Lee shrugged.

"As of tomorrow?"

"As of tomorrow." He looked unhappy.

"Dreams won't wait, Lee."

"No; they won't, will they?"

"I think it would be better if I went for her. I can talk with her. You go after him."

"You make it sound like a bounty hunt."

"It won't be as easy as that. Now, show me my room. It's late."

THREE

She had to move fast to be on time for the ferry. With about twenty minutes to spare she drove the Midget on to the boat at Stranraer, and was glad to get out to stretch her legs. After spending the night at Lee's flat she had driven back to her house in Cumbria, had a second bad night's sleep before driving hard to catch the boat to Larne.

Slipping out of the harbor at Stranraer, with the dockside diminishing with each blink, she felt the sea breeze stir around her and along with it came her first misgivings about what she was doing, doubts about her Northern Ireland mission. All her energies had gone into persuading Lee to trust her instincts and follow her lead. She hadn't thought to stand back and question her convictions.

She thought about Lee, at his house, wanting to kiss her. She had no illusions about it. It was an act of desperation. He thought that a renewal of their relationship would be a way of holding off terror; he wanted to distill from intimacy the bitter-sweet salve which offers protection.

Lee, stolid Lee, had lowered his eyes in an attempt to disguise a disappointment that would have been no more obvious if he had cried out loud and smitten his brow. He was too gentle to do anything but accept her rejection and retire to his bed, where he would curl up with his confusion. But in the night, when Ella had felt the bad dreams thickening around her like storm clouds, she had thought of Lee, lying asleep and vulnerable in the darkness of his room. So she'd confused him even further by going to him and slipping into his bed.

Lee had woken up to feel her next to him.

"I'm cold; go back to sleep." Which was what he did, happily; and for which Ella was thankful.

In the morning Ella had felt the muscular warmth of Lee's arms wrapped around her waist, though he slept on. She could feel his erection becoming hard against the back of her thighs. Sliding out of his unrestraining arms, she pulled on some clothes and opened the blinds. She put coffee on to brew and walked out of the flat, leaving the door open.

Lee was woken by the telephone. He looked around for Ella. He could smell the fresh coffee brewing.

"It's me."

"Where are you?"

"A hundred yards down the street. Thought I'd pull you out of it with the telephone. We don't want any bad starts to the day."

"You're a life saver, Ella."

"One day you might save mine." *Click*.

Lee had showered by the time Ella returned, clutching a bag of croissants. "It's good," he said. "I feel more confident this morning. There's a clarity which I haven't felt for a while. The smell of the coffee and the croissants. This is awake."

Lee's confidence brought a lot of things back to Ella. But if she suspected that it was neither coffee nor croissants that made Lee

felt stronger, she didn't say anything. Anyway, she had to agree
with him. It was true, there was a kind of sharpness, an extra definition about things today. Outside in the street she had sensed a
crackle in the morning air, and she had been confident that this
morning they would be untroubled by the nightmare procession of
false awakenings.

Experience told her not to waste hope on this respite. Yet it was
in that morning's spirit of optimism that they had drawn up their
campaign to contact the others. They had already agreed that it
should be Ella who would go to Northern Ireland.

Which was how she came to be standing out on deck on the ferry to
Larne. It was the last day of February, too cold to spend more than a
few minutes outside, too cold altogether for most people, which left
her with the deck to herself. Ella loved it, huddled in her flying
jacket, a bitter wind raking her hair, and the ferry dipping through
the spume of the waves.

But when the sky darkened to the color of a bruise, and the sea
turned black, her doubts started to thicken. She knew that the voy-
age would reawaken the one thing that she least wanted. The
thought sickened her. Then the wind picked up a foul stench off the
water. It was a whiff of corruption; a secret known only to the sea.

The boat rose and fell. Over the stern a ragged company of
grey-backed gulls wheeled and dived. But it was neither cruel beaks
nor talons, nor the gulls' greedy eyes that fascinated and terrified
Ella as she stared out to sea. It was the hovering nameless thing that
went scavenging and sucking at the wake of her journey, and in the
wake of the bad dreams that would come to threaten them all.

F O U R

Whither is fled the visionary gleam?
Where is it now, the glory and the dream?
—Wordsworth

This wasn't what he had wanted at all, scuttling around trying to track someone down without knowing if he was dead or alive, emigrated, gaoled, dropped out, socially elevated or just erased from the face of the earth; trying to find a character whose company he couldn't abide and who under normal circumstances he would cross vast deserts to avoid.

Brad Cousins. Where the hell are you now?

The trail was erratic. Ella had already exercised her powers by obtaining—against university policy—an original home address and telephone number in Sale, Manchester. It led to an odd phone call.

"Mr. Cousins? My name is Lee Peterson. I'm an old . . . friend of your son, from university days. I'm trying to get in touch with him." The line started crackling. "Do you know where I could get hold of him?"

"Nope."

"No idea?"

"I don't ask; he don't tell." Lee could hear the man's asthmatic breathing.

"Would Mrs. Cousins know?"

"She might; but she'll not tell; she's been dead six year since."
The line was beginning to break up.

"Where was he last time you heard?"

"Saudi . . . Germany . . . Yugoslavia . . ." He pronounced this
last with a 'J'.

"Can't you give me an idea?"

At last, and with an air of crushing uninterest, the man yielded
the name PhileCo, a Midlands pharmaceutical company his son had
worked for some time ago. From PhileCo the unpromising trail led
through four drug companies, for which Cousins had been a sales
rep in less than as many years. It ran cold with a West Country firm
called Lytex, where a chatty personnel officer admitted that, yes, the
man had been an employee of the company representing their prod-
uct to GPs in the region, but that after a few months of mediocre
returns he had stopped weighing in for work. Lee emerged from the
conversation with an address in Cornwall.

He made careful preparations, packing a double change of
clothes, a set of brushes, a travel shaver and a gift manicure set. A
manicure set? He wondered when he had become so fastidious.

He took the train to Plymouth, and spent the journey sipping
weak tea and gazing gloomily at the landscape. In the carriage window he had three or more ears, multiple eyebrows and chins to
spare. He almost liked himself better that way.

His thoughts turned to Ella. Their reunion had plunged him
back into the morass of his adolescent longing. He didn't know
whether to blame that on the dreaming or on Ella. He had hoped that
his greater maturity would do something to defuse the excitement he
felt in her presence, but just thinking about her made his cheeks burn.

She was a witch, he had decided. Or at least a mesmerist or a
spellbinder of some kind. It was Ella, after all, who had led him into
this whole bizarre situation. All she claimed to want was an end to
the dreaming. Yet he knew that Ella was notoriously unclear about
her own state of mind. She was not as in control as she liked to

appear, and he knew that, behind her assertiveness, she would be depending on his support.

Her behavior back at his flat had been ambiguous to say the least. She seemed to be signalling that she wanted intimacy, and yet she had kept him at arm's length. Then she had climbed into his bed half-way through the night, and he had had to pretend to be asleep to avoid making love to her. But at least since she had come his nights had been undisturbed by the repeated dream awakenings.

At Plymouth, Lee hired a Cavalier from a lady in an orange costume and lopsided orange lipstick (which made him think of Ella again). It was already late afternoon.

Dusk was settling. He drove out of town and crossed the Tamar bridge into Cornwall, heading towards Gunnislake. By the time he reached the village it was dark, and then he got hopelessly lost looking for his turn-off. Eventually he found it—hardly more than a dirt track—and arrived at two isolated cottages. One slouched in semi-derelict condition with a collapsed roof and broken windows; the second was in only slightly better shape. A bare light bulb was burning in a downstairs room.

He drove his car as close as he could to the front door. On a wooden plaque on the wall, weather-split and almost completely effaced, Lee could just about discern the word *Elderwine*. He sighed, less than happy that he'd found the place.

He switched off the engine and killed the lights. He sat for a moment, hoping that someone would appear. Then he got out of the car and went to the door. No one answered his knock. He tried again, waited, and pushed at the handle. The door swung open; a pile of unopened envelopes lay on the mat. They were addressed to Brad Cousins. Lee went in.

FIVE

For years I cannot hum a bit
Or sing the smallest song;
And this the dreadful reason is,
My legs are grown too long!
—Edward Lear

Ella, meanwhile, found her prey with relative ease. The ferry journey, the disembarkation and the drive down to Fermanagh had gone smoothly, and she was soon walking unchallenged through the doors of the primary school. Through a glass window in a classroom door she saw the woman she sought.

Honora Brennan was gathering up stubbed-out paint brushes and jam jars of murky water, offering words of encouragement after an end-of-day paint your fantasy session—yes anything you like, the sky the trees the stars at night. Is that the stars at night, she says to one seven-year-old with a pink NHS eyepatch, no he says it's the mortar that got me da, is it she says, put it in the pile with the others and wash out your brushes in the sink. On instinct Honora looked up and saw Ella watching her.

Briskly, she dismissed the class, then turned to rinse the paint-pots as if by this chore she could make the other woman disappear. Ella willed her to turn around: *Don't block me out Honora.* If Honora heard the words, she fought them.

"Yes, I'm here; you're not dreaming."

Honora stiffened, stacking the pots in a precise pyramid.

"How did you get here?" Her back still turned, she scrubbed at an already gleaming jar.

"You can still get a boat across the water."

"I'm sorry, Ella. I wanted to say 'It's lovely to see you' but I didn't feel it."

"Then you were right not to say it."

Honora busied herself thumbtacking the children's paintings to the wall. Ella waited.

"Do you know why I came?"

Honora looked into her eyes for the first time. "Can't we go somewhere?"

Outside, walking side by side in their thick winter coats, Ella was surprised when Honora gently linked arms with her. She remembered that type of endearing, girlish gesture so well; that, and a fresh smell of camomile and rainwater. Honora's tawny hair fell as it always had, into a tight nest of curls and ringlets. She exuded a vulnerability that made Ella, by contrast, feel coarse.

They went to a small tea shop and peered at each other. The window was misted with condensation. Every time someone came in or left, a door-shaped wedge of cold air sent a shiver around the seated customers. Outside a UDR soldier with his cockade feather erect patrolled by with that circumspect hip-swivelling security walk. Ella watched him.

"After a while you stop seeing them."

"Are we talking about soldiers?"

"What else? They look like shadows; but they're real."

"And what about the real shadows?"

Ella flattered herself that she always knew when someone was dissembling. She had an idea that she could peer, if not into a person's darkest heart, then at least into the blue or grey or green of their eyes, where she might detect the microscopic splash imperceptible to others. Honora dropped her eyes and tried to change the subject.

"You gave me the fright of my life when I saw you outside the classroom. I never expected to see you again, least of all here. It suddenly brought it all back to me. How we were and all that. Weren't we crazy then, Ella? Wasn't it all madness?"

"Oh yes, it was that all right."

"But it's grand to see you. Really it is."

"I wish you meant that." The remark made Honora look away again. "You know why I came to see you."

"You want to talk to me about dreams?"

"We could talk about the IRA instead. Or the Mountains of Mourne. Or about Donegal tweed . . ."

"All right, all right. So, let's talk about dreams. I'm happy to talk about dreams, if that's what you want me to talk about."

"I want to talk about the kind of things that happened to us while we were at university. I mean, if anything like that has been happening to you lately."

"Oh, come on Ella! Don't you think I didn't have enough with what happened at the time? I put it all behind me. I was glad to get away from it when I had the chance. And now it's all in the past."

"It's not in the past. It's back and it's not nice."

"But don't you see what it is!" Honora cried. "Just this talking about it is what does it. You're dredging it all up again. Why can't you leave it alone? The more you want to discuss and analyze and toss it back and forth the more you bring it all back again. It was a mistake, something we did when we were young. It's something we shouldn't keep going back to; like an old—"

"Like an old affair?"

"Something like that."

"Lee said some very similar things, about not wanting to open it all up."

"Well, he's right. Me and him both."

"But he's a different kind of person. Remember what we used to call *the repeater*? He's been having some of those dreams again. Only it's not a joke any more. Some mornings it's panic . . ."

"Are you living with Lee?"

"No, but I know what you're thinking, and you're wrong. We didn't get together and resurrect this dreaming thing. It started happening to both of us independently. I got frightened, so I got in touch with Lee. That was when I found that the same things were happening to him. I'd already decided that one of the original circle was muddying the pool; so if it wasn't me and it wasn't Lee . . ."

"You thought it might be me."

"I had to come and find you, at least. You can understand that, can't you?"

"Yes, I can understand it."

Dusk had rolled over the street outside the tea shop. A hand switched on dim lights. Now half of Honora's face was in grey shadow, the other half washed by unhelpful amber light. Another patrol passed by the misted window.

Ella was still trying to get Honora to pick up the ball. "So you haven't been troubled by any of that . . . weird stuff? No repeaters. No flashbacks. None of it?"

"Not at all." Honora's eyes were too wide open to be telling the truth.

"Never, over the years?"

"Not since what happened at university. For a year or two after that I did have the occasional nightmare, but that was more of the regular order of bad dreams. If you want my opinion, I'm glad I can't help you. It's dead and gone, and I'd like to keep it that way."

Honora said all of this too cheerfully, working a fraction too hard at trying to keep it light. She was smiling at Ella with those delicate features, but now she was looking like a toy left out in the rain. Yes; there was a pallor under the skin left by the sleeping pills,

Ella could guess that; but most revealing were the very fine lines, a tiny chain of folds in her skin which she saw as knives, daggers turned inwards on the subject.

"And over the years you've never had any contact with—"

"None." Honora cut Ella very short. "I don't even want to think about him, far less talk about him. Can we pay this bill?"

Ella sat back.

"I wasn't going to ask you to stay," said Honora with a smile, "but I can't really not, now can I?"

"No, you can't really not. We've got a hundred other things to catch up on."

They threaded their way through the streets of the town, Honora once again linking arms with her old friend. Her house was a two-up two-down brick terrace, its interior painted in bold primary colors. It was almost obsessively tidy, except in the back room which was cluttered with the unframed canvases and rolls of cartridge paper which Honora used for painting and drawing.

"In the summer I still go into town and paint portraits for American and German tourists," Honora explained. "And sometimes I get commissions to paint people's pets. Dreadful!"

"Stinking!" Ella agreed brightly.

One painting rested on a chair, draped with a chequered tablecloth. "Can I see?" Ella asked. But Honora ushered her gently out of the room and switched off the light. Ella suddenly knew exactly what lay under the cloth, as if she herself had splashed it on the canvas in luminous paint.

"What would you like to do while you're here?" Honora asked hurriedly.

"You mean apart from talking about dreams?"

Honora looked defeated.

"Why did you lie to me, Honora? You never used to lie."

Honora turned to the window. "All right, the dreams have been back. I don't even like talking about it. I don't know what's happened, why the . . . *repeaters* are frightening me again. I hadn't experienced them for over ten years. I thought you must have been doing something, perhaps you and Lee, cooking something up together, resurrecting the dreaming. I thought you might want to include me in some scheme or other . . ."

"I told you; Lee and I don't want it any more than you do."

"Oh I realize that now. But I just want to black it out, hide somewhere, not talk about it, not think about it. When you came I thought: Oh God no, this is why the dreams have been coming back, leave me out of it."

"Do you think us coming together can make things worse?"

"I don't know anything; it just triggers a lot of . . . associations."

"The point is, if it's not you or Lee or me, then it must be . . ."

"Yes. I was afraid of him. My God Ella, what's happening to us?"

Ella didn't answer. "We should go out tonight," she said, trying to brighten things.

"I never go out."

"You do this evening. I want Guinness and didley-didley music, and you can show me where to get it."

All protests were brushed aside, and Honora, who an astonished, high-spirited Ella later discovered hadn't been outside her house socially for two whole years, was dragged out in a state of excitement and nervous terror mixed. When they left the house it was snowing; soft, light flakes of snow falling under the amber streetlamps, melting the instant they touched the ground.

S I X

*If we swallow arsenic we must be poisoned, and he
who dreams as I have done, must be troubled*
—William Cowper

Elderwine Cottage, damp and stinking. Stooping to gather a fistful of letters franked more than a fortnight before, Lee yelled something intended to be Hallo or Anyone In but which came out unintelligibly between. Off right, a narrow hall of razor-edged shadows admitted to a room with a bare light bulb burning. He carefully nudged open the door. It was ankle deep in newspapers and litter. Some of the papers were unread and folded neatly in piles, some had obviously served as wrappings for a variety of take-away foods. Judging by the smell, some still did. Floating in the debris were dozens of brown ale and whiskey empties, bottles frozen neck-up in a polluted lake. In the next room he tried flicking on a light switch for a bulb that was missing. He passed through to the kitchen. A tinker's workshop of pans and dishes was stacked high in the sinkful of grey water, a half-inch slab of grease on the surface; rock-hard doorsteps of sliced bread grew fibrous green beards; disposable fast food cartons were left strategically, still offering half of their original contents; milk bottles stood with their contents crusting in phases of metamorphosis. It was more like a biochemist's laboratory than a kitchen.

"Brad Cousins!" He climbed the creaking wooden steps and

found upstairs two cold empty rooms with generations of paper stripping itself from the walls. Downstairs again, he took a second look in the back room with the broken light. There was a man asleep on the couch like a bundled sack, roped and tied at the top.

"Is that you Brad?" he said loudly. The sack didn't stir, but he knew that he had found his man.

Brad Cousins slept on, his jaw slack and his mouth open, a string of saliva swinging from his chin to his T-shirt like a delicate piece of suspension engineering. A pair of scuffed laceless brogues were kicked off at the end of the couch, adding to the general stench of lived-in nylon socks. From matted head to swollen foot, the sleeping body exuded a root odor, and a sweet-rotten scent of sweat and alcohol commingled.

"Brad. Brad, it's Lee. Lee Peterson."

One crimson-cupped eye opened. Lee found himself talking as though through a drainpipe. "Brad. I've come a long way to see you. I've come to talk to you, Brad. We have to talk. All right?"

The bloodshot eye glazed over, an inner protective membrane forming across it.

"Brad. I want you to listen, Brad. Can you hear me? There are some questions I need to ask you."

The eye closed. "No, don't go to sleep again, Brad. I don't want you to go back to sleep. Brad. Brad. *Wake up*, Brad."

This time both eyes opened and with a startling marionette movement he jerked himself upright on the couch. His eyes were like glass beads fixed on Lee. Finally he got up and lurched unsteadily out of the room. Lee heard him go out through the back door and then heard the clanking mechanism of the backyard toilet flush. He returned without a word.

"Brad. Listen to what I'm saying—"

"You have my permission to stop talking to me as if I'm in a coma," Cousins interrupted. "If I'm not saying much right now it's because I'm conducting a lively debate with myself. Interior dialogue. If the better half of me wins the debate, I'll go back to sleep. Then when I wake up you won't be here and I'll feel much happier."

"Don't count on it."

"OK, so why *are* you here? Let me run the options. I borrowed half a quid from you when we were students and you've come to get it back. No? Your marriage is on the rocks and you want some advice from your ol' mate Brad Cousins who always knew how to handle women. Yes? Or you need a career break and you want me to use my position to pull a few strings for you, is that it? Eh? Well I don't have half a quid, I never give advice and my influence is on the wane. You wasted a journey. You can go." He leaned back and closed his eyes.

"Just came to have a little talk with you, Brad."

"Are you still here? I thought I was only—"

"Dreaming?"

"What do you want?" Brad scowled, play-time over.

"The booze doesn't keep the dreams away, does it?"

Cousins got up and wobbled over to the other side of the room, steadying himself against a heavy oak sideboard. "Away at bay I pray they stay."

"You're still pissed."

Cousins drew a circle in the air and punctured it with a nicotine-dyed finger. "I'd forgotten how telepathically perceptive you were."

"Do you sleep well?"

"I sleep like a baby log. Thanks."

"No bad dreams?"

"Ah! Dreamscreams?"

"Any repeaters?"

"Dreameaters?"

"Ever go *back there?*"

"Dreamscare?"

"You like this game?"

"Why not. How long can we play?"

"How long can you keep it up? How long can you go on pretending?"

"You were always boring; did I ever tell you that? Always boring."

"Why won't you talk about it?"

"*It*. What is *It*, exactly?" The cabinet door in the sideboard had lost its handle. Cousins expertly prised it open with his fingertips. He lifted out a third-full bottle of Scotch and a dusty, gluey-looking tumbler with a long human hair, probably his own, stuck at the rim.

The whiskey splashed into the tumbler as if it were Cola. No companion drink was offered. "*It* is an unappreciated visit from an unwanted past. *It* appears when you're least expecting *it*, and when you least want *it*. *It* comes when you are asleep, when you thought you were enjoying yourself, defenses down, getting in the zeds. *It* knows that *it*'s not welcome, but *it* sits there uninvited in your comfortable squalid little nest with *its* ridiculous mouth open asking for answers to questions."

"I can't say that age or booze has had a mellowing effect on you."

"Mellowing? Spare me. You've come to discuss my spiritual development."

"People like you don't develop; they ferment. I've come to talk about *dreaming*."

At that last word, Cousins moved to the window, glass in hand. He leaned against the window-sill and peered over at the neighboring tumbledown cottage. "No, don't change the subject. Really. I'm always interested in your observations concerning my moral and social progress. Who will you be reporting back to, I wonder."

"I've seen Ella, if that's what you mean. That's why I'm here."

"How is the old slag? Has she slept her way to prominence? Good luck to her and all who sail in her." He seemed to have spotted something and leaned toward the window.

"What about you?" Lee trying to be barbed in return. "Did you ever see Honora Brennan again?"

Cousins tried to spit out the hair that caught in his mouth. He kept his back turned as Lee spoke. "You know why I came here. Someone's been stirring things up. Now either you've been *back there* muddying the water, or if it's not you, then at least like Ella and myself you've been caught in the backwash."

"What can I do against such dazzling logic?"

"You can drop the act; you're as frightened as we are."

"Aw, shaddup."

"What are you afraid of? Don't want to be reminded of what happened back there? Don't want to remember your special part in it?"

"All right! All right! I did go *back there* as a matter of fact. I didn't want to go. In fact I tried bloody hard not to go. I spent night after bloody night fighting to keep it away. But it was too strong. It got so I was afraid to go to sleep at night, because I knew what was going to happen. I used pills to stay awake three or four days, and then when the inevitable happened I didn't have the strength left to resist it." He turned to face Lee across the room. "You wouldn't recognize the old place now: they've got penny arcades and fat lady shows, and hot-dog stands and end-of-pier comedy acts. It's quite a tourist pull these days; you should get Ella to go down there with you for the bank holiday."

"You're scared, Cousins." Lee stood up. "You live ankle deep in shit and you're scared. I can smell it on you, even through all the booze."

"And I don't even owe you the time of day!"

He turned back to the window. Lee was at a loss. Swaying uneasily against the unlit fireplace, he rubbed his hand along the dusty mantelpiece, waiting for resolution to materialize out of nothing. Cousins nodded at the crumbling cottage across the yard. "She's out there. I've seen her."

Lee stepped across to the window. He could see nothing.

"Who? Who are you talking about? Ella?"

"Noooo," waving a finger at the dereliction. "Not Ella. Her."

"There's nothing. Nothing."

"Did you see that? Did you see that light there—just a flicker. You couldn't have missed it. Did you see it?"

Cousins's gluey eyes were pressed against the window. He stank. Lee stepped back, looked around at the filth and debris of the room, wondered what he was doing there. There was no trace of light in the other cottage. He had had enough.

"To hell with it. I didn't see anything. And I'm going. I shouldn't even have come."

It was as if a spell had been lifted. He was appalled that he had allowed Ella to pack him off on this fool's errand. This confrontation disgusted him. But what really vexed him was not that Brad was a sot but that there was something about Brad's slither into alcoholic slush that was only superficially different to his own dash for stiff conformity. Both of them were casualties—Ella's word for it: men whose souls leaked through the corrosion which followed brilliant dreaming.

Now Ella had got him scurrying down here rattling chains and locks that were turning to dust in his hands. He felt alone, he wanted his neat home, his hermetically sealed box, wanted not to be confronted with this degenerate version of himself where the only distinction between them was a full set of buttons and a splash of cologne.

"You can . . . put your head down here for the night . . ." Cousins said, suddenly sheepish.

"What?" A mirthless laugh. "Is that a funny? Thanks, old friend, but no thanks. I'll take my chances of roughing it at The Plough, back down the road."

Back behind the steering wheel, he turned his headlamps up full on the derelict cottage. He had let Cousins spook him. He could still see him watching from the window. Turning the car around rapidly he drove back on to the road, switching on the wireless for the comfort of a Radio 4 voice.

At the Plough, with barely more customers than staff, he had no difficulty in getting accommodation for the night. He was shown to a room with an uneven floor and heavy Victorian furniture. Before turning in, he opened a window and looked out across the moonless, starless valley, wondering why he had bothered to come, but already knowing the answer. In the comfortable bed he fell into a fitful sleep; a seamless patchwork of dreams crossing easily from past to present and back again to the past.

PART TWO

April 1974

ONE

Remember not the sins and offences of my youth
—1662 Prayer Book

LUCID DREAMERS
Lucid dreamers are subjects who, while dreaming,
are also capable of becoming aware that they are
dreaming and in certain cases capable of controlling
the direction of their dreams. Volunteers who have
experienced this phenomenon are required to partici-
pate in practical research experiments under the
supervision of the Department of Psychology.

The poster, hand-written in bold red marker pen, was displayed
in the main university concourse, and Lee was pretending to read it.
He was pretending to read it so that he could stand next to Ella, the
girl with the spray-on blue jeans. She was also studying the poster,
and he had to strain to hear the words she was speaking to her friend.

Lee stood close enough to take in her scent of patchouli, baby
soap, unruly pheromones and warm apple-blossom skin. He had
spotted her once before, in the university library. He'd been dozing
over his reading, and his first sight of her had been enough to make
him leave toothmarks in De Quincey's *Confessions of an English
Opium Eater*. How was anyone expected to study?

So when he'd seen her here he'd had to go and stand behind her. He still hadn't thought of anything sparkling to say, when she turned from the poster and walked right into him.

"Sorry," he said. It was his best line.

But she and her friend had gone, leaving Lee defeated and slumped against the noticeboard. When he recovered he was able to read the poster for himself. He thought he was probably not a lucid dreamer (whatever animal that might be), but he had heard Ella saying that she was going and guessed that he could always do a good job of pretending; at least until he was found out, or for as long as it took to get on coffee-bar terms with Ella, whichever came first.

So why not? He set off across the university lawns. Spring was on him like a drug, as if the air was full of music, there until you tried to stop and make it out. Spring in the air, like the confirmation of a rumor.

Lee arrived at the small seminar room in a state of high anticipation. About a dozen people, none of whom he knew, sat around in a rough circle. Ella wasn't there. They sat whispering to each other while on one isolated chair, hands folded on his lap and gazing with expressionless interest at the floor, sat the Head of the Department of Psychology, Professor L. P. Burns.

Now nearing retirement, Burns had led a distinguished but unspectacular academic career, making a number of suitably perplexing contributions to educational psychology and parapsychology, although he always maintained that the latter interest ranked only as a hobby. He wore a drab mottled green suit. His hair was thin and his skin stretched like parchment across his face, but his eyes were moist and alert, and the angular characteristic of his features dissolved easily when he smiled.

Lee was already thinking about how he could get out of this when the professor suddenly spoke as if he were addressing a full lecture theatre. "It is some five minutes after the appointed time. I don't think we are going to be joined by many more, given that we compete with the thousand and one delights offered by the university on such a spring evening, so we will make a start. But even as I speak I see I am to be contradicted. Come in, ladies, do come in."

Two girls hovered doubtfully behind the open door—Ella and her companion. They stepped into the room. Ella wore a black beret and black tights, and took a seat opposite Lee, crossing her legs as she sat down. Lee crossed his.

"Excellent," declared the professor, passing a list around the circle for everyone to sign. "This is almost a better turn-out than I get at my lectures." A polite titter went around the circle.

"Are any of you psychology students? I don't recognize anyone." If any of them were, they didn't own up.

"Excellent again!" said the professor. "We might just get some intelligent contributions." Another polite titter, dying after a single circuit. "So, you are all lucid dreamers? Yes? No? You all spend your nights dreaming lucidly in your beds? Yes? No?" He looked around jovially from face to embarrassed face. With no answer forthcoming he continued. "What is required is a corpus of willing volunteers, such as yourselves, prepared to take part in a scientific, accurately documented piece of research into the interesting subject of lucid dreaming; a phenomenon which, however commonplace it may seem to you," he smiled at Lee, "is not, after all, experienced by many of us. I for example am not a lucid dreamer. Unlike you I have never experienced the what to me would be thrilling prospect of controlling, manipulating, directing or merely influencing the course of my dreams; nor even the sensation of knowing that what I am experiencing is a dream, and of therefore being able to say to myself that shortly I will awake from this dream into another reality."

"Excuse me," a girl with an Irish accent said shyly, "I'm not sure whether I'm a lucid dreamer or not."

"We'll come on to that," said Burns. "What I would like to establish first is whether the people here would be prepared to make

the necessary commitments involved. The research must be scientif-
ically handled and this will involve keeping diaries of your dream
experiences, the introduction of certain exercises into your dreaming
and the faithful participation in a weekly evening seminar, hopefully
in more convivial surroundings than this, for the further discussion
and exploration of your respective dream studies and experiences.
Of course this will require a certain discipline, something which I
find to be rather a dirty word amongst today's students."

Another snigger went around the room, but it was arrested at
the boy sitting on Lee's immediate left, a dark-haired youth with
deep-set eyes and a chinful of stubble. "How much will we be getting paid?" he demanded.

"A good question. Let's clear that up without further delay.
And you are . . . ?"

"Brad," said the boy, rather taken aback at the professor's smiling response, "or rather Brad Cousins."

"Well now Brad, or rather Brad Cousins, we must get that matter straightened out before there is any confusion. I hope not to dis-
illusion you by saying that there is no payment. No, on the contrary,
the principle involved is similar to that of the donor system at the
medical center; only it's not your blood or your semen we are after,
it's your dreams."

This time a laugh did a couple of circuits. Brad shrugged.

"For incentive," the old academic continued, "the departmental
budget might be seen to extend to the provision of a glass of wine
and a dice-shaped piece of cheese or two at our weekly gathering,
and possibly even to an end of term dinner party; beyond that we
offer but the thrill of the intellectual hunt, in the hopefully not vain
speculation that Mr. Cousins and the rest of you will be stimulated
and satisfied by this more metaphysical payoff."

"Glad I don't have to go to his fucking lectures," Cousins whispered at Lee.

Lee broke his gaze, which had hitherto been fixed on the tiny Himalaya of Ella Innes's kneecap. Ella's own attention was concentrated upon the professor, and her face had already assumed the irritating expression of the disciple at the feet of the avatar.

"Let's see what we've got," said the professor clasping his hands together and indicating the person on his right. "Let's go withershins—why do you think you are a *lucid* dreamer?"

Each person was invited to summarize their experiences. Lee was relieved that he was not obliged to go first. Most simply declared that they were often vaguely or partially aware while dreaming that they were in a dream state. One or two sometimes felt able to influence the direction their dreams were taking. Ella spectacularly declared that she had, on occasion, been clearly able to control the course of her dreams, but she was outdone by Brad's contribution, for it was Brad who asserted, almost with disdain, that he was sometimes able to reactivate a dream from a previous night.

"Like putting a tape into a cassette," said Burns.

"Almost," said Cousins.

"I think I'm probably a possible lucid dreamer, or perhaps a half-lucid dreamer," said the Irish girl.

"I think it probable that that's possibly enough for you to be of great interest to this company," Burns replied, with exaggerated gallantry.

When it was Lee's turn to speak, with all eyes sharply focused on him, he became acutely self-conscious. Ella leaned forward, her lips parted and her eyes expectant—a solicitous fascination she had offered to all contributions short and long but which touched him like acid on litmus. He parroted a few words stolen from one of the earlier speakers, unexciting remarks about occasional awareness. Ella fell back in her seat. Lee felt as though he'd had his testicles calibrated and was found lacking.

"But I do sometimes have premonitions," he almost shouted as an afterthought, hoping the lie would rekindle some interest. Lee glanced over at Ella. It had done the trick. She smiled at him briefly.

"A different matter," said the professor, "but one which I predict will be interesting to test."

"Would you mind if I talked to the chaplain before agreeing to go ahead with these experiments?" asked one girl. "Only I would like his reassurance that I'm not, you know, *dabbling*."

"Dabbling? Hmmm. Talk to the chaplain by all means; I'm sure he will let you dream with his blessing." The professor suppressed a smile. "Any further questions? None? Good. Start keeping a diary of your dreaming. I don't want you to do anything unusual, just make a daily record of the scenario and figures of your dreams. Concentrate on detail. I want no interpretation, thank you very much: Messrs Freud, Adler, Jung and all those other old bores are not invited to the party and will be regarded as gatecrashers. For this week I simply want you to find your way into the habit of recording. That's all. Nothing arduous in that. You may or may not find that this in itself begins to have an effect. If you don't dream, write clearly in your diary that you were unable to recall your dream but that it is your intention to recall subsequent dreams. A small tip: set your alarm clocks half an hour earlier than you normally wake. We will, if at all serious about this, make a few sacrifices. We shall meet at the same time every week, for a slightly longer period, having more to talk about. All clear?"

Everything was clear.

"So." The professor got up and walked to the door. Before closing the door behind him he turned and looked back. "Sweet dreams," he said darkly.

The students pushed back their chairs and made movements towards the door.

"Anyone going for a drink?" Brad shouted.

"I could go for that," said Lee, looking encouragingly towards Ella and her friend.

Ella, along with the rest of the students, shuffled out without replying. Bollocks, thought Lee.

TWO

Youth, which is forgiven everything,
forgives itself nothing
—Shaw

Brad Cousins was exercising his favorite habit of speaking to one person as if they were a gathering of ten. Lee was his audience. Against the backdrop of the student bar, pinball tables chattering, crack of pool balls striking and muted Stones' classics piped through a stuttering PA system, Lee was regaled with an accumulating list of Brad's personal antipathies. He was half-way down a pint of flat amber beer by the time he had been instructed on Brad's aversion to basketball, brazil nuts and beehive hairdos, his detestation of Liverpudlians, lavender perfume and looseleaf ringbinders, his hatred of trade unions, tapioca and television journalists. Lee groaned inwardly at the thought of another dismal half-pint's worth of cataloguing before he could make his excuses and leave.

"She's dirty," cackled Brad, breaking off from his inventory of rancor, "I like her; dirty."

Lee followed Brad's gaze and locked on to a figure in black beret and black tights standing at the bar. Having shaken off her shadowy friend, Ella Innes had arrived and was ordering herself a drink. As she turned from the bar Lee semaphored wildly to attract her attention. But she looked through him without recognition, and

settled at a nearby table where she expertly proceeded to roll a cigarette in brown liquorice paper.

"Frosty," Brad scoffed, swirling his beer to make it froth. "Anyway I can't stand women who drink out of pint glasses to try and
prove something."

Lee ignored him. Ella's table was two strides away. "I waved at
you to ask if you wanted to join us," he said, sitting down next to her.

Ella moved an eighth of an inch away from him. "Yes, I saw
you." She concentrated on crafting the cigarette in her long white
fingers, only looking up at him as she slid her tongue along the
gummed edge of the paper.

"Oh?"

"Pardon?" She blinked at him.

Lee hovered, looking for a way out. She's pulling my strings, he
thought. "Why don't you join us?"

Ella looked over her shoulder as if for signs of imminent rescue.
She was an international celebrity being pestered for three minutes
of her time by a provincial journalist. With a practised, long-suffer-
ing *if there's to be no help* shrug she gathered her papers, matches,
tobacco and beer and relocated to their table.

"What did you make of that session?" Lee asked.

She shrugged and lit her cigarette. "What did you?"

"That beret is ridiculous," Brad said to ten people. "You look like a
member of the Provisional IRA. In drag. After a bad night. In Belfast."

"The thing about going to these sessions," Ella said to Lee, "is
that you never know who you're going to meet."

Brad pretended that the irony was lost on him. "All I'm saying
is that the effect doesn't work. It doesn't come off."

"I was interested," Lee cut in quickly, "in some of the things you
were saying. About controlling the direction of your dreams, I
mean. I'm really going to get into it."

"Do it," she said, as if to say stop talking about it.

"You sounded quite advanced."

"Head of the coven," said Brad.

"But I don't have premonitions." She plucked a loose flake of tobacco from the tip of her tongue.

"He only said that about premonitions," Brad put in, looking at Lee, "so he wouldn't sound as boring as the others. Isn't that right?" Lee only glared back at him.

"Ignore it," said Ella.

"And it worked," said Brad.

"What did you think of L. P.?" Lee asked her.

"I've come across him before; I think he's sweet."

"Why do women always say sweet when they mean clapped-out and half-way to senility?" Brad again. "What on earth is sweet about that dry old stick?"

"It's true," she replied drily, "that he doesn't suffer fools gladly."

Lee established that Ella was prepared to take the weekly sessions quite seriously. She told him that it hadn't occurred to her that most people were unable to direct their dreams. She was prepared, she said, to take things as far as she could to find out what they meant.

"I'm not," said Brad. "You sound like you're expecting too much from it. I can't see it going anywhere."

"Then why don't you drop out of it?"

"I probably will after a while."

"The group," said Ella to Lee, "would never recover."

She produced her purse to buy another drink. Lee offered twice, but she insisted that she buy her own. While she was away at the bar Brad said, "Listen mate; she's making you dance."

"What?"

"Dance! Dance! She's a vixen."

"A vixen? I don't know about that, but she's got you taped."

"Not a chance! Anyway it's not *my* tongue that's hanging out drooling: you're making an indecent public display of yourself."

"What?"

Brad got up to go. "I'll leave you to it." He patted Lee on the face. "Dirty."

Ella returned. "Your friend's gone, then?"

"I only met him tonight. He's not a friend."

"He's a reptile. He's got the eyes of a lizard and scales on the inside of his mouth." She crossed her legs.

"I see."

But Ella obviously didn't think of Lee as a reptile, otherwise she wouldn't have taken him back to the house she shared with two other girls about a mile from the university. Lee, for his part, overestimated Ella's style. Once they were behind closed doors he half-expected, wished, hoped that Ella would tear off her erotic black outfit and demand that they make urgent love (beret remaining in place). To say that Lee was more relieved than disappointed when she didn't would be a lie. He was a knot of tension and in Ella's presence his mouth ran dry. Although he was not a complete stranger to the private rooms of the women students, something about Ella's aura—a subtle scent and a kind of leading signal beyond the range and faculty of human definition—intimidated him while at the same time snaring him in a noose of sexual longing.

Ella at twenty was busy cultivating an air which, ten years later, she would be earnestly trying to throw off—that of the jaded adventuress, physically satiated, spiritually exhausted. This blasé image had, as was intended, a contradictory energizing effect on Lee. When he breathed in a single hot draft of this distillation of elements, it worked on him like a witch's potion. He perched nervously on the corner of her bed nursing a chipped mug of chicory-flavored coffee as she relaxed back into a comfortable armchair, crossing and uncrossing her legs.

Ella's room was a revelation. Those of other female students had always been pale stereotypes of pastel shades, feminine pillow-slips and obligatory postcard collections. Entering Ella's room was like walking into a subdued decorated cave or a Bedouin tent. The four walls were draped with hanging fabrics, Indian batiks, Serbian rugs, Greek blankets, Russian scarves, antique lace cloths—a hanging exhibition of textures, a treasury of intricate folds. Slow-burning incense breathed seductive fumes from elaborate brass cups. Ella relaxed in her armchair, rolling herself another liquorice-paper cigarette as she spoke. In Lee's mind she had already fused the mystical qualities of the Tarot Priestess, a 1970s Sibyl, and a contemporary Circe into one exotic being, and had focused them all into a soft dark triangle at the top of her legs.

"I don't do drugs any more; it's a waste of spiritual energy," she was saying. She seemed to be deliberately parodying herself.

"I've come to the same conclusion," said Lee, who had never so much as abused the instructions on an aspirin bottle.

"I'm in and out of TM at the moment . . ." she continued.

"TM?"

"Transcendental Meditation."

"Right."

"Only just recently I got my head into TA . . ."

"TA?"

"Transactional Analysis."

"Right."

"Where've you been living?" asked Ella.

"I've been into TP."

Ella looked foggy. "TP?"

"Teaching Practice. TP. It's a joke."

"A joke," said Ella. "Right." She looked at her watch and glanced at the door.

"You're quite a spiritual entity," Lee tried. It was obviously the right thing to say. Ella brightened, or perhaps her aura expanded, but anyway she proceeded to map out the dizzying geography of her psychic development over the past twelve months. In a matter of minutes she alluded to astrological configurations and Zen Buddhism; the Tibetan *Book of the Dead* and Hexagrams of the *I Ching;* Tantric Lore and Cabbalistic Law; primal screams and astral projection; rebirth experiences and regression into former lives.

Lee thought he might be talking to a Martian.

"In the end you're just chasing your tail," said Ella. Lee nodded in sage concurrence. "Which is why I'm interested in this dream thing. I want to leave all that clutter behind, trust in my own resources. I want to get inside my own head."

I just want to get inside your pants, Lee thought. "Exactly why I'm interested," he said.

Coffee had gone cold in the bottom of cups, incense had burned itself out. Ella was silent for the first time since they had walked through the door. Lee tried to keep the conversation on the boil by casually declaring that he was thinking of dropping out of university so that he could travel overland to Tibet.

"Do it," she said simply. It was the second time she had used the phrase that evening. There was something dismissive about the way she said it which twisted the knot in which she already had him tied.

Lee sat squirming on the corner of the bed, trying to think up a way of making the next move when she suddenly said, "Now I'd like to go to bed."

Lee stared at her, dumbfounded. Was that an invitation or what? He made an assessment of Ella's breezy self-confidence. "OK," he said, and started to untie his shoelaces.

Ella watched as he kicked off his shoes. Then she spoke.

"What the hell are you doing?" For a moment she looked flustered and a little wide-eyed: an apprentice Sibyl lost for words, a novice Circe frightened by a piglet.

"You don't want me to stay?" asked Lee.

"If ever I do," she said, recovering slightly, "you'll be the first to hear of it."

Lee pulled his shoes back on, trying to model a win-some-lose-some look as Ella opened the door. At the last minute she tore a book from the shelf and thrust it into his hands, simultaneously propelling him forward. "You really must read this and let me know what you think of it OK goodnight." She closed the door just a little too hurriedly behind him.

Lee took a short cut across the university lawns, philosophical. The book Ella had given him must have been a way of saying that the door would be open another time. He was half-way home before he looked at it. It was a battered paperback copy of *Alice in Wonderland*. The university clock-tower rang out the hour in the distance. It was 2 A.M.

THREE

Why, sometimes I've believed as many as
six impossible things before breakfast
—Lewis Carroll

The silence was embarrassing. The second meeting of the lucid dreamers had convened in Professor Burns's own lounge in a large house close to the university and across the road from a sprawling Victorian graveyard. They had turned up at staggered intervals, and after being warmly greeted by the professor were seated in one of the assorted armchairs drawn into a circle. Lee arrived late and suffered agonies on seeing Brad Cousins ensconced on a small, cosy-looking sofa with Ella Innes. Lee took a seat next to the shy Irish girl.

"Had any premonitions?" she whispered as soon as he sat down.

"Not one."

At last the group became aware that the professor was patiently awaiting their silence so that a start could be made. The whispering diminished in tiers until they were left gazing upon Burns, waiting for session number two to begin. But he didn't speak.

The professor remained with his gaze fixed steadily three feet above the head of a girl immediately opposite him. His face carried a perfectly neutral expression, neither hostile nor friendly, neither impatient nor uninterested. Fidgeting began and increased as the period of silence extended. A sigh, a scratch, a cough, the sound of someone twisting in their seat all punctured the embarrassing hiatus before it was immediately sealed up again with silence. After an agonizing five minutes of nothing, Brad Cousins spoke.

"If this is a psychological exercise designed to make us all feel uncomfortable, it's working."

All eyes were turned on the professor, who did nothing to acknowledge the remark or deal with the implicit criticism. His expression remained consistent, as did his gaze. The group, exasperated, plunged into a silence more oppressive than the last. The silence seemed to expand, becoming more profound as it lengthened. Lee looked at Ella; Ella looked at Lee. Brad looked at Ella and Lee; Lee looked at Brad. The Irish girl looked at Lee; Lee looked at the Irish girl, Brad and Ella. Ella looked at Brad, Lee and the Irish girl. Now no one seemed to want to look at the professor at all, except sideways.

"If nothing's happening," Brad tried again, "maybe we should all go away and come back next week." His words fell like the sound of a small pebble tossed into a vast reservoir. Now everyone, with the exception of the professor, affected to be fascinated with their fingernails or their footwear.

At last, but not before the agonized hush had become a rack upon which everyone lay stretched, the professor spoke. "It might or might not be," he intoned, "that in fact a great deal more is happening in this group than if we were to pretend otherwise by speaking." A few there nodded heads in counterfeit sagacity; others looked around wildly for help. The pressure of the silence was redoubled.

He looked gently at the Irish girl sitting beside Lee. "Honora is it? Did you dream, Honora?"

"I did dream," said Honora, "and I was aware that I was dreaming."

"So you are now a card-carrying lucid dreamer. Did you keep a diary?"

"I did." Honora produced an open black ring-binder in which Lee could see large copperplate handwriting interspersed with fiber color or lead pencil drawings. "I also made a few sketches of . . . situations . . . if you can call them that."

L. P. Burns was impressed and said so. He proceeded around the room, pressing everyone on the subject of diaries, which appeared to be more important to him than the cargo of dreams they carried. Lee claimed to have forgotten to bring his.

"Forgot?"

"I didn't realize we would be needing them tonight," he said lamely.

"Even with your special foresight?" said the professor.

"Sorry?"

"Never mind. Next." He made the word sound like a bell.

Brad Cousins declared with a proud swagger that he hadn't had a single dream since the last meeting of the group, not even the night he got roaring drunk.

"Perhaps you're blocking, so that you can't remember."

"I don't think so; I don't want to miss the fun."

"But your largely unconscious reasons for blocking," said the professor, "might not find the dreams all that amusing."

"Possible."

"More than possible; believe it." The professor fixed his eye on him until Brad was forced to look away.

Another student digressed on her history of migraine and treated the company to a dismal saga concerning repeated visits to the health center, including names, dates and times of day, in order to obtain prescriptions for sleeping pills of different varieties all of which failed in turn to produce the desired remedy. Burns listened patiently before moving on to Ella. Where the last speaker had numbed the group, Ella startled them into life again by bravely declaring that all of her dreams had been of an exotically sexual nature and that her self-awareness during the dreams had been acute.

"Funky!" yelled Brad Cousins, cutting Ella short.

"I'm not entirely sure whether Brother Cousins intends to encourage you or discourage you with that last shouted remark," said the professor, "but we might all feel relieved to remember that our interests are more concerned with levels of awareness than with precise anatomical descriptions."

A stifled giggle did the circuit before Ella protested, "It's just that I can be choosy about who I do it with!"

"Whom!" yelled Brad, trying in vain to whip up a group guffaw. "Whom you do it with!"

The professor leaned in towards Ella, and so did the rest of the group. "Can you genuinely control who takes part in your dream . . . *encounters?*" he asked.

"Sometimes; not always. Faces slip and change; it can be an effort to keep things fixed."

"Sounds like it's an orgy!" Brad Cousins being helpful again.

Burns held up an admonitory hand to Brad as he pressed Ella further. "You are actually conscious of an effort, a struggle to direct the dream along a course predetermined by yourself?"

"Yes."

"Struggling agaisnt what, exactly?"

"Well; against the natural flow of the dream."

"So you could make the choice to *sit back* as it were, and experience a different dream over which you would have no influence?"

"Yes."

Silence, as the group watched the professor turning over the possibilities of Ella's revelations. They waited for the nugget of his profound deliberations. "Sounds like pretty sophisticated stuff," he said.

Ella flushed her humility, uneasy at being rocketed to the top of the class.

At the end of their discussions the professor set an exercise.

"Homework," said Brad.

"Yes, Brother Cousins," said Burns, "dreamwork. Continue to keep a meticulous record in your diaries. But now I have some exercises for you which may or may not lubricate the passage through to lucidity, by which of course I mean they may facilitate lucid dreaming; you too Ella, notwithstanding your superior control.

"Exercise one: ask yourself several times through the course of your day whether or not you are dreaming. I am sure that many students in this university if confronted with the same question would have difficulty in replying within a time period briefer than fifteen minutes, but I have nothing but faith in all of you here. Is it a matter of some amusement Messrs Cousins and Peterson? Good; be amused, but do it. And the second part of that exercise is, having persuaded yourself that you are not after all dreaming, to go on to tell yourself that you want to recognize and be aware of the fact that you are dreaming the next time a dream occurs. Clear?"

"Can I ask myself," said Brad, "if I am dreaming that you are really saying this to us?"

"Very witty, Brother Cousins, well done. Of course I don't mind where you ask it so long as you complete the exercise as I have described. The principle is quite simply that of leaving your unconscious mind so many messages and memos that it will eventually have to act on them.

"Exercise two: next time you wake up from a dream, try to imagine yourself going straight back into that dream. And when you are back in there, at least in your imagination, instruct yourself that the next time you dream you want to be aware of the fact. Tell yourself that you want to recognize that you are dreaming. Thus in approximating the dream state you are making your intentions very clear. More memos to yourself. That's all. As I said, keep a record of all of this and indeed of your ordinary dreams."

"What if you're not having any dreams?" asked Brad.

"Correction: what if you're not *remembering* any of your dreams. You need to know that if you're not remembering your dreams when you wake up, it is probably because you don't want to remember them. For some reason you are blocking the recall of those dreams. I don't know why you would be doing this; you must ask yourself. It may be because something in the dream frightened you and you don't want to remember it. Perhaps the dream contains a message asking you to change something about yourself that you don't want to change. Or you may be terrified of being in an environment where you are not in control of what is happening. Or perhaps you are just preoccupied with too many other things. I don't know. If this is happening to you, ask yourself why."

"Very helpful," Brad whispered to Ella.

"I'm sorry if I can't work this out for you. What I will say is that you will recall your dreams not through an act of willpower, but more by letting go. That is why I said that all you can do is leave messages around the place for yourself. Does that make sense?" Brad screwed up his face. "No? Something for you to think on. Meanwhile keep your diary by your bedside, and on waking scribble the first things that come to your head. This might give you some access to dream material. Try waking up after sleeping for a multiple of one and a half hours, which is the normal time between dreams. In other words if you go to sleep at midnight, wake at seven-thirty, not at eight o'clock; or in Brother Cousins's case at nine or at ten-thirty or whatever part of the day you can manage. Finally, last time I told you to set your alarm clocks to wake you up, but I want you to begin to train yourself to wake up without the intrusion of an alarm. This is because it causes a radical change of consciousness which I want you to avoid. You must learn to surface with your dream. Any questions?"

There were none.

————

The post-session analysis took place in the nearest bar. Lee, Ella and Brad had been joined by the Irish girl, Honora, and two other members of the group. Brad was complaining loudly.

"He's just taking the piss out of us. Seems to me that he's got us there under the pretext of doing something about this dreaming crap, while he's really using it for some other kind of study which will no doubt distinguish his own academic career and make monkeys out of us."

"He puts you in your place at any rate." Ella, with her head down constructing another of her liquorice-paper snouts.

"We wouldn't expect complaints from the prima donna."

"But we would," light, puff, puff, "expect them to come," puff, "from the clown prince."

"Never mind Ella's pornographic fairy-tales," said Brad, "what was all that crap at the start of the evening?"

"Perhaps he was just trying to create an intense atmosphere," said Honora.

"To make the dream stuff seem more real," Ella agreed.

"That's probably it, *Brother* Cousins," said Lee, raising a laugh.

"You'll agree with anything she says if it'll help you get into her pants," said Brad. Lee groped for the laser riposte, but it wasn't there.

"Looks like we've found our lowest common denominator," said Ella.

"Lowest what? You were the one who turned the discussion into a blue movie."

"You have to be honest if you're talking about dreams," Honora said angrily. "You shouldn't abuse people's honesty by taking advantage of what they say in the sessions."

Brad lamely mimicked Honora's soft Fermanagh brogue. "Would it be the priest or the professor gave you that idea now?"

"Honora's right, we've got to have confidentiality," said Lee decisively.

"So you're after the Irish one as well, are you?"

"If you intend to get fucking mouthy about personal things said in the sessions no one's going to open up. That's the point."

Brad, taken aback by Lee's sudden aggression, shrugged. "I didn't realize we were such a *serious* bunch of kiddies."

"We are," said Ella, "is the point."

"Yes, we are, is the point," said Honora.

F O U R

Only people with no imagination
have to resort to their dream life
—Fransisco Umbral

The dreamwork seminars continued, measured against the advance of spring. Lee persevered in a knot of frustrated lust for Ella and blamed this condition for the temporary abandonment of his studies. The late night sessions in Ella's room continued, but they never brought him closer to her. Ella usually invited Honora and other people from the dreamwork group back to her draped cavern, where he had to satisfy himself not with the hot, honeyed sex of fantasies, but with fluting, undergraduate conversation and a long stick of hand-rolled tobacco which supposedly contained something interesting, but which only ever burned his throat. Even Brad Cousins, who was always patently uninvited to these sessions, often managed to insinuate himself into the barricade of languid bodies that blocked any prospect of physical intimacy with Ella.

Against all contrivance, Lee always seemed to find himself sitting opposite and away from Ella, a kind of dumb agitation corrugating his brow as he fidgeted and gazed over at her. She would sit on the floor with her legs drawn up under her and lecture someone—probably about the coming revolution—while making gentle karate chopping motions at the air in front of her as if she were neatly slicing her argument into digestible chunks. Occasionally,

just occasionally, she might look up and grant him the special intimacy of a brief smile. Like any starving man, he showed a pathetic
gratitude for these meager crumbs.

On the rare moments he did find himself alone with Ella, he
balanced himself on the edge of her bed like a jungle cat waiting to
pounce but never feeling that the moment was quite right. After the
initial mistake he had made on the first night, he felt sorely inhibited. In any event, in the absence of a crowd of bodies, Ella set up
another kind of barricade—an unbroken mesh of words; a tirade of
original ideas, rehashed theories, speculations and unproven asser-
tions which constituted her semi-occult excursions of the past or her
left-wing projections for the future.

"I'm a fucking revolutionary," she said, on many an occasion.

Once Lee, who knew different, decided to throw down the
intellectual gauntlet. "No you're not," he said.

"Yes I am."

"No you're not."

"Yes I am."

"No you're not."

"Why am I not?"

"You're just not."

"Why not?"

Lee got out before things got too deep. "Never mind."

Nothing much was happening. And it wasn't happening in Lee's
dreaming activities any more than it was happening in his sex life. In
fact he couldn't see much difference between the two. Both seemed to
involve some futile speculation which was failing miserably to produce
dividends, and he had almost forgotten what one had to do with the
other. He persisted with the prescribed exercises whenever he remembered what they were, earnestly quizzing himself about whether or not
he was dreaming and solemnly reminding himself to become aware
during his next dream. But these exercises were always broken by sexual fantasies of architectural proportion, with Ella Innes as the central

pillar. Conversely, the most potent of these fantasies of Ella would occasionally be startled by the flashing thought that he must by all means become aware during his next dream. As far as he understood it, the relationship between the two things, sex and dreaming—and he was honest enough to recognize his own motivation—was that if he did manage to control his dreams, then in that other shadowy place he might have more success with Ella Innes than he did in the real world.

He continued to attend the dreamwork sessions, conscientiously reporting complete inventions. He was smart enough to make only the most modest of claims, in case he was pressed for detail by the professor. At times he considered dropping out, as some others had done, but then, in one session, Ella crossed and uncrossed her legs and he remembered why he was there.

"Dreamwork," said the professor, breaking into Lee's reverie and signalling the end of the session. "Awareness of dreaming, in at least some muted form, is now upon most of us, so I have another exercise for you. I want you to perform this exercise at every opportunity during your dreams. Look at your hands in front of your face. Try to fix your gaze on your hands. Look at your hands and try to hold them there for as long as you can manage. That's all."

One night, shortly after that session, something strange happened. Lee was asleep and dreaming. In the dream he met not Ella, but Honora Brennan, the Irish girl from the seminars.

Lee found a small walled garden in the middle of busy streets. All around it, giant concrete towers loomed, and above it was a colossal motorway flyover with loud, but somehow distant, rush-hour traffic. The garden had been planted between two of the flyover's huge pillars. In its center he came across Honora sprawled in a deckchair and wearing a thin cotton dress. In the telepathy of the dream both recognized the erotic effect this dress was having on Lee, and Honora seemed to flaunt the fact that she wore nothing underneath. Honora seemed relaxed, Lee felt uneasy. Slowly, Honora rose to her feet, then climbed the one tree in the garden to sit on one of the lower branches. Clamping her legs, she let herself fall backwards, so that she dangled upside down, hanging from the clenched backs of her knees. Her dress slipped down over her naked body, revealing a pubic bush of shining chestnut curls above her flat, white belly.

"Do you know you are dreaming?" she asked Lee.

"I know it."

"Remember your hands." And Honora disappeared like the Cheshire Cat.

He raised his hands and looked at them for a long time, until he grew bored.

On waking, Lee scribbled everything down, and even prepared a dummy back-diary so that he would have a respectable document to present at the next seminar. He reported the dream faithfully, omitting just a few of the erotic elements, and sat back to be congratulated.

A number of the initial participants had left, including the girl with migraine, who claimed that the exercises exacerbated her medical condition, and the girl who had consulted the chaplain only to find that the dreamwork sessions clashed with the Christian Union's candle-and-guitar nights. The group now comprised only "graduated" lucid dreamers with established credentials. To most people's dissatisfaction Brad Cousins was still a regular and was now dreaming, as he said himself, with Technicolor lucidity.

Lee's excited report was greeted with a mild response. He was merely showing signs of catching up with the rest. "Why," said Burns, sensing Lee's frustration with the obduracy of the group, "would you consider this experience of lucidity to be of greater significance than any of your experiences hitherto?"

Lee was in no position to admit that his "previous experiences" were woven of a fabric even thinner than dreams. "Obvious," he said, claiming time to think.

"This obvious factor," Burns twitching one of his secret smiles, "is a mite too slender for my apprehension. Would you like to share it?"

"It seems to me that people in the group have begun to help each other in this enterprise, perhaps unconsciously."

Some eyes squinted in appreciation of this idea and some heads nodded. Burns thought for a moment.

"Interesting proposition, Lee." The professor's familiar address was new. "But I would tend to be more modest about claiming the erotic or otherwise attentions of the admittedly attractive Miss Brennan. I think you can safely claim this to be your own work."

Heads nodded, some nostrils snorted, all in agreement with this sound judgement. Embarrassed but not offended, Honora smiled timidly at Lee. But if his new powers failed to impress the group as a whole, they had an interesting effect on Ella.

After the session, as the reduced group trailed out of the professor's house, Lee hung back to talk with Honora, worried that he might have embarrassed her by blurting graphic descriptions of her lurid behavior in his dreams. But his concern also had something to do with the fact that the intensity of his dream had conferred an enhanced radiance on Honora. She *looked* different.

It was while Lee was talking to Honora that Ella dropped back and inserted a proprietary arm under his.

"I just told Brad and the others that we were going on somewhere," she said.

"Oh," said Lee.

"Right, then," said Ella.

"Right, then."

For a moment they stared dumbly at each other.

"Next time," said Honora, already a shadow hurrying to catch the others.

Lee and Ella walked along the side of the cemetery as dusk fell, then out across the park towards Ella's house.

"Where is this somewhere we are going?"

"Nowhere different," said Ella, "I didn't want to do the usual; chew the fat, all that stuff."

It was a mild spring night. When they reached the row of cherry blossom trees by the tennis courts, Ella stopped abruptly, and turned and kissed his lips. She quickly slipped his arm, skipped away from him and leaned against the bough of one of the trees.

"That dream," she said.

"What?"

He took a step towards her but she reached up for a low branch and scrambled up to sit on it. She looked back at him. Her eyes were like gleaming obsidian and her hair fell across her face. She was a spirit in the tree.

"Do you know what I can do?"

"What can you do?"

"I can do this."

Clasping her calf muscles tight against the branch she let herself fall backwards, hanging from the backs of her knees, swinging slightly as she dangled there upside down, her hair falling away from her ears and neck, her outstretched arms almost reaching the grass.

Lee was mesmerized. "Yet it's not the same."

"Do it."

Lee put his hand on her stomach, creamy white in the darkness, and unbuttoned and unzipped her faded blue jeans. He undressed her against gravity, pushing up her jeans and pants to her knees to reveal the upward-pointing black triangle of hair, where in the dream he had wanted to put his tongue, and where here he did so. Ella shivered, and asked him to lift her down.

They walked across the park to Ella's house, most of the way in silence. When they got there Ella made her room even more like a cave by switching off the lights and lighting candles and turning the place into a flickering nimbus of joss scents. Only then would she let Lee undress her, this time with gravity in support. She pulled back a sheet on her mattress on the floor. Lee thought he might be dreaming, but he wasn't.

F I V E

Romeo: I dream'd a dream tonight.
Mercutio: And so did I.
Romeo: Well, what was yours?
Mercutio: That dreamers often lie
—Shakespeare

Two episodes of explosive excitement had been touched off in Lee Peterson's life, one seeming to detonate the other. In the daytime he and Ella skipped lectures in favor of a program of sexual exhaustion, Ella's acrobatic invention matching Lee's ardor. In the nights which followed, either with numb satiated bodies entangled as they slept or with restless limbs disturbing all deep sleep when they lay apart, Lee found his awareness during dreaming beginning to grow. He was able to arrest the progress of ordinary dreaming whenever it occurred to him to look at his hands. From that moment he would always know he was dreaming, and that he would shortly wake. From this awareness he progressed rapidly to a level of control over the substance of his dreams of which he had previously thought himself incapable. In the dream state, the awareness of hands turned into simple exercises recalled from childhood but generating profound excitement:

Here is the church here is the steeple
Open the door and here are the people

It was as though he had opened a real door to a parallel physical dimension, a door through which he could actually pass. These hand manipulations gave way to the conjuring of small objects from nowhere, like a stage magician. In the dream it was possible to make a silver coin, a rubber ball, an ace of spades appear. The objects which could be summoned were limitless; the only difficulty was to sustain control. A kind of forgetfulness would take over him after a few seconds, a veil would be drawn over the lucidity and control of the dream, and all would be lost as the dream shifted or stopped.

Lee made copious notes in his dreamwork diary and told Ella everything, as if he were passing on hard news. Ella listened intently to his feverish reports, nodding occasionally but neither probing into these accounts of his abilities nor inviting comparison with her own experiences. Indeed, Ella stopped remarking about her own lucid dreaming experiments beyond the reports which she reserved for the formal dreamwork seminars. Meanwhile, Lee was in a state of high excitement, massively stimulated by the curiously related developments now pushing back the boundaries of his experience. The bouts of lucid dreaming had an aphrodisiac effect on him and Ella reciprocated time and time again with unwavering energy. In turn the dizzying sex sessions acted like a thunderous backdrop to Lee's dreaming, an amphetamine boost to his struggle to assert control over the substance of his dreams. It was a struggle in which, step by tiny ominous step, he felt himself nearer to victory.

The weekly meetings of the lucid dreamers continued, and Lee became one of the most dedicated and most vocal attenders. Professor Burns could always be relied upon to smuggle some new box of tricks into each session. At one meeting he introduced the practice of dreamwork re-entry, an attempt to reactivate a dream in which lucid dreaming had taken place by using relaxation techniques and the gentle guidance of his semihypnotic prompts. There were some successful results in reactivating dream associations in this conscious state, but the main requirement for these sessions was for the group to create a hypnotic atmosphere of stillness and peace. There was one main obstacle to this:

"I can't help it; when everyone goes so quiet and po-faced I just want to laugh." Brad had spent an hour in the bar before the session.

"We will allow you a minute or two to giggle it out of you Mr. Cousins." Burns was beginning to lose his secret smile at this third interruption. "And then we will try again."

"Doesn't anyone else see the ridiculous side of it?"

"No. Only you." Lee had become Brad's sparring partner in the sessions, but at this remark Brad started snorting again, pretending to suppress his guffaws by stuffing a grimy handkerchief into his mouth.

"Couldn't we etherize Brad and use him as a subject for re-entry?" Lee was serious.

"Rear entry? Not my line, mate."

"Ether is a very old-fashioned method . . ." said Burns.

"But we share the sentiment," said Ella. "What about carefully placed electrodes?"

"Mind-expanding drugs?" suggested another, warming to the subject.

"Too ambitious," said Ella.

Brad snorted derisively.

"If we're finally ready to start," said Burns, "let's have Honora."

"Let's have Honora!" shouted Brad.

"That's enough vulgarity," Burns retorted sharply.

"Rear-entry!" countered Brad.

"I think all of the assembled company would deeply appreciate it, Mr. Cousins," said the old professor in his most formal voice, "if you would be so kind as to shut your consummately tedious gob."

The session continued in peace.

————

Sleeping alone that night, dreaming his bauble-juggling tricks, Lee got a whiff of some of the possibilities of this *dreamshaping*, as it had been dubbed. He began to feel the potency of his control and was ready to try something new, a major progression, like conjuring another person to his dream. But suddenly, his grip on the dream loosened, not by loss of concentration as usual, but by a sound like hail on a tin roof. The sound woke him and he realized that some-one was rapping frantically on the window of his cell-sized room.

"What does it take to wake you up? Let me in, I'm soaked."

"It's four in the morning Ella, what are you doing?"

"I'm standing in the rain trying to bloody well get in!" Ella's hair was plastered to her head, raindrops bubbled on a face red from running, blue from cold. She wore a long raincoat, collar turned up and clutched at her throat. "Jesus! Let me in!"

"Yes right. I'll come round and open the door."

"Just push the bloody window up."

Ella half-climbed half-fell through the opened window, bring-ing with her fresh grass cuttings pasted to her boots and the smell of spring rain. As she kicked off the boots Lee could see that she was wearing nothing beneath her coat but her knickers, which she threw off before leaping, shivering and complaining, into his single bed. Lee climbed in with her.

"You're as cold as the grave, Ella."

"Never mind that," teeth chattering, pressing herself to him, "it happened and I ran over to tell you."

"What happened? Ella, you ran two miles practically naked in the pouring rain in the middle of the night, what for?"

"Can't you guess?"

"No."

"Guess!"

"You're not—?"

Ella thought. "Christ no, I'm not *pregnant*; I wouldn't tell you if I was!" Lee felt a thin shadow of disappointment. "I came to tell you about the dream I had. I mean the lucid dream, it happened, I *made* it happen."

"I don't understand."

"I made it happen. By myself. I did just what you described, with the hands, I made objects appear in my hands in the dream, and then I made them go away again."

"What?"

"What, what?" Ella mimicked heavily.

"But what about all the other times." Lee sat up. "All your other lucid dreams. All that stuff in your dreamwork diary. All those lurid accounts you gave in the seminars."

"No," pinching his nipple between her teeth, "this was the real thing!"

"The real thing? What was the other stuff then?"

"It was . . . not the real thing."

"Wait a second. You mean you made it up?"

"Sort of."

"What do you mean sort of? You don't sort of make up things like that! You mean it was all lies. Jesus! *All* your stories of lucid dreams were all a pack of lies."

"Not exactly lies. More kind of half-lucid dreams."

"Day dreams more like! It was all bullshit!"

"Don't get so fucking superior—you've only just started lucid dreaming yourself, remember! You strung people along at the beginning."

"But not with Technicolor big-budget cast-of-thousands porno-graphic epics like yours! Christ I believed every word; so did all the others. I'm going to enjoy telling them. I'll enjoy telling Brad!"

"You won't say anything. The important thing is that it really happened. I *made* it happen."

"I'm going to tell them all! Miss Lucid Dreamer of the Year! I can't wait to see their faces!"

"You won't tell on me," said Ella. She took his cock in her cold hands and rolled it like dough. Rain swept against the outside windows in great gusts, coming in through the open window, soaking the curtain and dampening the disorderly heap of books.

"Here is the church," she said, "here is the steeple."

He promised not to say anything.

S I X

Learn from your dreams what you lack
—W. H. Auden

From that night Ella stopped her I'm-more-lucid-than-you games. She was a fast learner, and her genuine skills developed accordingly. She contrived to disguise the substantial change in the accounts she offered to the weekly seminar, and if anyone was made suspicious by her later reports being more modest than her early claims, nobody said anything. Even so, an unacknowledged hierarchy did develop in the group, with Lee, Ella, Brad and Honora clearly emerging as the people with the strongest ability to influence the course of their dreaming. Each of them progressed, without major effort, from being able to conjure small objects to switching locations and settings in which dreaming took place.

Professor Burns, when pressed, admitted that, despite several years of trying, he, like most people, had never experienced the state of self-awareness during dreaming which would allow him to manipulate the course of dream events. "I think I'm too crusted over by a life devoted to academic pursuits," he confessed, admitting to more than a little envy of their abilities. "Besides which," he added, "I don't have the modern swagger of youth in the face of fear."

End of term beckoned, and the round of dreamwork seminars was held to be a moderate success. Their efforts, Burns asserted, while not having lit up the skies of science and progress, had contributed to a growing body of research in the increasingly important field of parapsychology. To conclude matters, he added cheerfully, a miserly wine-and-cheese celebration on the expenses of the parsimonious departmental budget would be arranged for the final week of term.

The students made their arrangements for a long summer: Ella and Lee planned a backpacking expedition around the Greek Islands, sleeping on beaches and living on tzatsiki and feta cheese salads; Honora a trip home to beautiful County Fermanagh where she hoped to make a few pounds sketching portraits of tourists boating on the loughs; while Brad, as a medical student, had work which would keep him at the university. Meanwhile June warmed the nights in which they lay in their beds and dreamed their lucid dreams.

Invitations to the wine and cheese party came as promised. The students dutifully spruced up and went along to the house. A stiff performance with an early finish was predicted, but they were surprised to find Professor Burns racing around in high spirits, his eyes enlivened by whatever share of the drinks he had already consumed, exhorting everyone to get stuck in to the crates of wine that had been provided along with the standard party fare of cubes of cheese and French loaves.

"Drink! It'll probably be the last time we can get this out of the miserable blighters!" Burns danced around, lavishly topping up any glass within arm's length, everyone's congenial host. "Don't be shy Brother Cousins, there's another crate through there!"

Some group members had brought their partners, swelling the numbers to twenty or more young people freely availing themselves of the generous flow of wine and filling the house with noisy chatter. Burns held forth to a knot of students in the corner, his steady stream of university anecdotes and outrageous disclosures producing waves of raucous laughter. After an hour or so he noticed Honora standing alone in the middle of the room with an empty glass. He cha-cha-cha'd his way over to her. He had obviously been making the most of the departmental wine while the going was good. His jewel eyes blazed merrily and a long thin lock of iron-grey hair had become displaced from its habitual coiled groove across the top of his head. It hung gamely down the side of one ear.

"Wait behind, Miss Brennan," he whispered as he refilled her glass of white wine from the bottle of dry red he was carrying, "after all the others have gone." He winked, then cha-cha-cha'd back to the corner of the room. Honora, speechless, coloring, looked around to see if anyone else had noticed. Ella drifted by.

"L. P. is pissed," said Ella.

"I know; he's trying to chat me up."

"No! What did he say?"

"He wants me to stay behind afterwards."

"Then we're in for three-in-a-bed; he asked me to stay, too."

"What *can* he want?"

"We'll probably have to suck his balls."

"I'm not going to!" cried Honora.

"No, don't," said Ella, already regretting the joke. "But he's a sharp old cookie. He must be up to something."

Ella knew that Burns had also invited Lee to stay. She had a sneaking suspicion that Brad would also be asked. Indeed, when Burns shepherded out the last of the guests, Brad was still looking very comfortable in a large high-winged armchair, nursing his very own wine bottle. Honora looked deeply relieved.

"Yes, help yourselves to that; I don't really want the incriminating stuff hanging around here." Burns was carrying out empty and half-empty wine glasses four in each hand. Then he returned and closed the door behind him. "I did intend," he said, holding out his glass to Brad, "to keep a clear head, but the road to Hell blah blah."

"Blah blah." Brad poured from his bottle, stealing a glance at the others.

"Quite right. Point being, why did I ask you four to stay behind?"

"Because we four are your most lucid dreamers—we've got nothing else in common."

"Too right," someone else agreed.

"Too right indeed. But the question is are the four of you interested in continuing?"

"Continuing? Continuing how?"

"Yes, Ella, continuing. Carrying on," said Burns as if he was having to explain an obscure concept or an arcane word, "progressing, doing more, not stopping, going further. Some rather more intensive exercises, under more testing conditions, exploring the true potential of these . . . talents of yours."

"Sounds interesting," said Lee, "but I'd got the idea we'd taken things as far as they could go."

"Oh, I don't think that's the case at all. Remember, it wasn't until half-way through the seminar program that you discovered your capacity for lucid dreaming." Lee looked at Ella. "Likewise Ella. Come on, don't look quite so sheepish. It's not important; I know your later accounts were genuine enough. What I'm more concerned about is whether you four will stay on over the summer vacation and do some real work."

"The thing is," said Brad, swirling wine dregs in a smeary glass, "we don't all have the luxury of the academic cushion."

"Pardon?" Burns's eyebrows were twin Norman arches.

"He means some of us have to spend the summer working," said Lee.

"I thought of that. And not wanting any of you to suffer the indignity of having to work for a living, I thought of a way of keeping you on as temporary research assistants. At least until the new term begins. Of course I'd want some results out of you; but from what I've observed of your academic activities, Brother Cousins, it won't squeeze out your studies."

"You mean we'd get paid?"

"A grant?"

"For *dreaming?*"

"And for writing up your results with a little more rigor than we've seen hitherto."

"What do you get out of it, apart from seeing your name under an article in *The Spoonbender's Gazette?*"

"Let's say, Brad, that I'm easily satisfied."

"Done," said Lee.

"Done," said the others.

"Good," said Burns, getting out of his chair, "next week we'll see if we can't start a program of *real* dreaming."

Ella was the last to file out through the hall. The door stood open to admit a wedge of cool night air, and a glimpse of a new moon hanging low over the graveyard opposite. The light played without sympathy on the old academic's cable-veined forehead as he helped Ella on with her coat.

"By the way," shaking her hair free of her collar, "how did you know when we, that is Lee and I, started lucid dreaming for real?"

"Oh," Burns smiled slyly, closing the door to behind her, "I'm a sharp old cookie."

SEVEN

All would be well
Could we but give us wholly to the dreams
—W. B. Yeats

"How do you mean, 'meet up' with each other?"

Term was over, the students had all gone home, summer was
delivering its promise. Lee and Ella had abandoned their plans for
combing the Mediterranean beaches of the Aegean islands; the
plump faces of German and American tourists went unflattered by
Honora's quick pencil sketches; and Brad's medical tomes lay
unstudied on the shelf.

The sash windows of Burns's lounge were pushed up to admit
the sweet summer air. Lee held out a hand for one of Ella's hand-
rolled liquorice-paper cigarettes which he had taken to smoking,
and Ella grudgingly passed him the one she had just been about to
light for herself. Honora reclined in a heavy armchair, her cotton
dress sticking to her moist skin as she fanned herself with an Erich
Fromm paperback she had plucked from the professor's shelves.
Brad looked on glumly with his eyebrows raised in the expression of
barely tolerant boredom that he had cultivated of late.

"I mean exactly that: arrange a meeting, a rendezvous between
the four of you at some pre-arranged location, just as you would in
normal waking life."

"Can it be done?" Ella, not looking up from her tobacco.

"It's already been done," Burns said impatiently, "many times, under laboratory conditions."

"If it's such a well-trodden path," said Brad, "why are we bothering to do it?"

Burns, looking tired, rested his head against the wings of his armchair. "I don't care to continually justify my interests; if you want my rationalizations then you'll have to earn them. If you do manage to rendezvous in dreamtime"—Burns used the new language, the conspiratorial argot of this small cell of lucid dreamers, *dreamside dreamtime dreamwork dreamthought dreamspeak*, to reaffirm his membership of the group—"then exchange a phrase, a song or a proverb. Something you can bring back as an objective correlative. Confirmation. Words that will become real things in waking time. That's all for tonight. Thank you."

He rose and escorted them to the door.

"Tetchy." Brad spoke against the background of a pulsating pub jukebox. "Very tetchy."

"You have that effect on people," said Ella. "In any case, it's time to move this thing into a different gear. Let's agree a rendezvous point, a meeting location which we could head for during dreaming. L. P. says others have done it, so why don't we give it a serious shot? We all manage to shift locations in dreamtime; let's agree on a place to meet."

"There's a difference," Brad muttered, "between shifting locations inside our own dreams and in bringing four different dreams together."

"It can work; I know it. I just know it." Honora surprised them with her enthusiasm. "Have faith. Just choose a place."

They all stared back at her, and for the first time Ella recognized the attraction which the Irish girl held for the two men. She saw them watching as Honora shyly averted her eyes and lifted her glass to her mouth. Honora was the one who talked least about the dreaming, who was the least inclined to speculate, but Ella sensed that she was also the one who dreamed deepest. She spoke as if she knew the coinage in that strange, different country. Ella warmed towards her and felt saddened by a simultaneous pang of jealousy.

"Honora's right," she said, breaking the spell, "we've got to believe it to be possible. If you've got any more doubts, Brad, keep them to yourself."

"Choose a place," Honora repeated.

Brad tapped the table in front of him. "This pub, preferably after hours when we can help ourselves."

"Be serious."

"I am being serious!!"

They walked home across the park. A full moon sat low in the sky. They walked past the tennis courts and along the row of cherry trees that some weeks ago had hung heavy with pink blossom. Brad aimed a full-throated howl at the appalled moon.

"This would be a good place to meet in dreamtime!" Ella still had strong associations for the place, as, she knew, did Lee.

"Are you sure?" said Lee.

"What's so special about this place?" Brad wanted a more dramatic setting.

"It's easier to make an outdoor scene appear than it is to shift to an indoor location."

"Is it hell," said Brad.

"Anyway this place has a certain intensity."

"Maybe it has for you two," he smirked. "It certainly does nothing for me."

"What do you mean by 'intensity'?" Honora wanted to know.

"It probably means they fucked here," said Brad. "But that's no help to us two."

"The place suits me," shrugged Honora. "Seems as good as any."

So a plan was formed and the group went their separate ways, hoping to meet there again, but in very different circumstances.

Brad insisted on walking Honora home, against all her protests. Ella saw Lee watching them go.

"Poor Honora," he said.

"Yes."

The night was hot. They propped the windows open with text books, but even then the air was close and uncomfortable, making sleep difficult. They lay on the mattress, discussing the night ahead. What would be the possibilities if they did rendezvous in dreamtime? Excitement kept them awake. Eventually, sleep took them.

Lee awoke with Ella leaning over him.

"Did you dream? Did you go there?"

"No," Lee still dazed, blinking stupidly, "I didn't even dream."

"Me neither. Nothing."

"Maybe we tried too hard."

"Maybe."

EIGHT

*To dream of creeping up a mountain signifies
the difficulty of the business at hand*
—Astrampsychus

For some time the project was a singular disappointment. Not only did the four fail to keep their dreamside appointments, but the dreams themselves failed to come. Or at least, they couldn't remember them in the morning. Whatever the reasons, they felt as if a power had suddenly been switched off at source, a cable disconnected, a fuse blown.

They tried a number of strategies to reactivate the circuit, all of which proved futile. Ella and Lee tried sleeping apart; another night Ella disappeared and returned an hour later with a small brown wedge of hashish in the hope of encouraging vivid dreams; they tried a program of rampant exhaustive sex, which, while enormously enjoyable, remained sadly ineffective; and they began a regimen of difficult-to-digest foods last thing at night, strong cheeses with exotic names and an array of pickles, all of which produced nothing more than bad breath. Finally they had to conclude that dreams rode on horses which, while they could be led to the dark waters of sleep, could not be made to drink.

Honora and Brad, inquiries revealed, were having similar problems. Nothing was happening. Honora, however, had a different theory about why her dream diary was gathering blank pages. She complained that Brad Cousins had taken to inviting himself back to her room every night for the past week, flatly refusing to leave until the dew was up on the grass. Honora's device for beating back his advances was to make a fresh mug of coffee every twenty minutes so that she might have something—a caffeine curtain—to draw between them. These massive doses of caffeine and the attendant lack of sleep did no more to remedy Brad's or Honora's current dream amnesia than any of the desperate nostrums employed by the other two.

"Let's run through all of the original exercises," said Burns, "from the beginning."

Ella stifled a yawn. They met more frequently now, and always at Burns's house. If they had thought that the extended 'grants' which Burns had miraculously engineered would promise them an easy summer, they had been mistaken. Burns proved to be rigorous about punctuality at meetings, exhaustive in his questioning and insistent upon meticulously kept journals charting the daily progress of their dreamwork. "This is not like studying for a degree," he said more than once, "this is real work."

Burns was trying hard to give them some uplift to beat the sag in the development curve.

"But we've been through all of those exercises," Ella protested. "That's not what's blocking things."

"So what is, exactly?"

"I don't know."

"Precisely. You don't know. I don't know. We all don't know. So we go back through it again, from the beginning, following our previously successful formula until something breaks for us; and what's more, we keep a diary every day charting the exercises and the results."

"But there are no results!" said Lee and Brad in chorus.

"So we carefully chart our exercises and note that there are no results, and we explore our lack of results. What's the matter with you?" Burns's exasperation was becoming more apparent. He marched over to the sash window and pushed it open.

"It's boring," said Honora.

"Oh! I do apologize if this scientific method of research is not a glittering parade of fun and spills involving one big kick after another. Pardon me." He sat down again abruptly.

"That's not what I meant."

"Then why say it?" The four stared glumly at the carpet. "So, as I said, we return to the beginning, repeat our original procedure and generate a new level of lucid dreaming."

Ella muttered something under her breath.

"Yes Ella, I know that you all belong to the Me generation and that you are accustomed to having everything you want exactly when you want it, instant coffee, instant money, instant gratification, a spoonful of this, a splash of that. Well let me tell you that this thing damn well won't make like that do you see? It's something you have to actually work for and only then might it work and even then only *might*." He got up again and stormed over to the sash window, this time slamming it down. "Now I think you'd all better go since you're not in the mood for work. Come back tomorrow when you're ready to be serious."

They walked slowly to the end of Burns's street, an avenue of three-storey houses with great gables prodding at the dusk.

"What's getting to him?" asked Ella, affecting cool but obviously stung.

"Maybe we asked for it," said Honora, stopping at the corner.

"Naw," said Brad, "he's just a constipated old grump who didn't get his dish of prunes today."

"We should be more methodical," Lee cut in, "if we're serious about it."

"Doesn't matter how serious," said Ella, flushing, "I can't dream to order. You don't turn dreams out like butterfly cakes hot from the oven; you have to wait until they come to you."

"Ella's right," said Brad, "what does Burns know about it? We're the ones making and delivering the goods, he's just the warehouseman with a pencil behind his ear hassling us about his invoices."

The post-mortem went on, with Honora and Lee becoming divided from the other two in an unnecessary defense of Burns. Then Lee began to mistrust Brad's motives and Ella to suspect Honora. It also caused some resentment between Lee and Ella, and neither desisted from tapping home the wedge that they set up between themselves. It seemed at times like these that the dreamwork project had become a vain and profitless obsession.

"Why did you side with her?" Ella asked Lee as they made their way home.

"I didn't side with her; she was right."

"That's the same thing."

"I just think we shouldn't play at it."

"Which means what exactly?"

"I think it needs a serious edge. Some of us aren't making the effort, and that's what's holding us back."

"And you think I play at it?"

"Sometimes; yes."

At that Ella turned away and walked off. Lee pretended he was not concerned, a self-deception that lasted five minutes. He thought he could punish her by not running after her. So he went home and got into bed alone, lying sleepless in the shadows, suffering agonies about where she was and what she was doing and whether she was with someone else. Then, after a few days, when he thought she had been punished enough, he went to her, to be readmitted to the scented cave, where he sulked for a few hours until their differences were forgotten. At least for the time being.

NINE

*But to withdraw one's steps and to make a way out
to the upper air, that's the task, that is the labor*
—Virgil

Burns, locking up after his students have gone, anticipates Ella's question seconds before she delivers it to the others as they dawdle on the street corner only yards away. He shakes his head. Exposing the students to your tantrums won't help anything—neither you nor them nor the project. It just makes you look as though senility is right behind you, pulling faces and drooling toothless for their entertainment. Anyway, what is it, exactly, that's eating you?

He returns to his study—a desk at the window and three walls of books on shelves so high he has to keep a footstool to reach the top. Not that he has reason to return to the tough-bound uppermost volumes, or those on the lower shelves for that matter, but the stool gets used by the lady who cleans and keeps house for him three days a week, since he happens to think that dust gathering on the ridge of untouched and out-of-print books symbolizes in too sharp a sense the slouch of old age into weak-mindedness and dotage. So he pays someone to come in and keep his books free of dust and his windows clean, so that the outer condition might at least reflect the preferred impression of the inner. So what's all this raving at the students, he asks himself.

It is early, still dusk, the students having been chased away by an infantile temperament, by his inexcusable tantrums, who was it this time, yes, Ella, who he hopes will forgive him quickly but who he knows is more sensitive than she pretends. He sits in his chair and takes his notes out of the top drawer, determined to log his observations even if the students are proving restive, but leave them, give 'em a break, they're young and full of it whatever it is, while he is feeling increasingly tired as he turns the pages and the pencil in his hands begins to scuttle across the blank folio leaves at high speed depositing a fine trace of lead in erratic bursts of what must be English but looks something like a fusion of bastard Arabic and autodidactic shorthand, and which for an account of an evening's research in which nothing is supposed to have happened and nothing is purported to have been done still manages to break across the page like the waves of the sea under a bracing wind.

He scribbles like one in the grip of a spirit, but it's nothing like that, being only too conscious of anything he might commit to paper and anyway too self-possessed to admit the intrusion of any second authority, from the spirit world or otherwise, to come between him and his outpourings. Tired, tired indeed, but hands still scuttling across the page at speed laying down a pattern of new ideas, complete and half-complete thoughts, perceptions, reminders, references and observations, all of this operating independently and at a level beneath or above his reproach of his own behavior, where he looks even now for a reason for his irritation and finds, depressingly, none other than that general malaise for which physicians have never found a satisfactory term other than old age.

Burns pauses and gazes out of his open window, blinking at a darkening horizon, dusk leaking from an unseen puncture in the silk and sable canvas, falling with defiant slowness but relentlessly enough, like the minute hand on the clock. He switches on an Anglepoise lamp which throws a ring of yellow light around his notes. He breathes in the sweet air of the summer evening and his hand automatically begins to scuttle back and forth across the white expanse of the page.

Not as if, he reflects, he doesn't prefer the company of the young students to that of the dry or childish presence of his academic colleagues. Because it is true he does prefer the buzz of youth and always has, three cheers for that, and what's more always dreaded turning into the crabbed old stick he felt himself becoming. And certainly these four were no worse than any others, and on the contrary he felt a special warmth for all of them, believing,—and perhaps this was the secret of what it was that was actually driving him harder and causing him to want to push them faster—believing, in a way that could never be more than intuitive, that there really might be something happening with these four, something in the chemistry that existed between them, something which he had sensed in the earlier seminars and the close comparisons in the nature of their results, just a spark, nothing rational, not yet anyway, but a spark and a shadow of apprehension—let's not call it fear— which had surprised him one day on recognizing the undercurrents in their respective commitments to this dreaming business.

And there was another problem, since the project had originally been double-bottomed, a smuggler's suitcase, the lucid dreaming project the ostensible reason for the seminars (and always a legitimate area for study, the dreaming project, since it was yielding up fascinating data) while Burns's other interest was a certain interactive study in the evolution and dynamics of the group. This covert study had of course never been made known to the seminar dreamers in the interests of protecting behavior from the influence of observation, the spyhole staying open as the group reduced to four participants for the same parallel purposes; but now the dreamwork study had begun to eclipse the other. This had also taken Burns by surprise, shocking him in that his impatience with another's small disinclination towards scientific method had caused him to cancel a whole evening's work on dream research.

But he knew that the current halt in progress, the vacuum in dreaming, was only a temporary arrest, a block that would be overcome by a little effort, put there by some external factor like the change in dynamics from the original large group to the group of four, or something happening between the four themselves. Whatever the block was, it would dissolve, and dreaming, strong dreaming, would resume. He had, he assured himself once again, a feeling about this group.

Burns's hand stops its mechanical movement across the page, and he drops his blunted pencil. He coughs, recovers, and presses a thumb and forefinger to his tired eyes. Always, and always at night before concluding his notes, he thinks, in an abstracted tender way, of his wife Lilly. It has been over a decade since she died, leaving a huge absence in his life, and one which he has only ever filled with a devotion for work of the kind he used to reserve for her. He leans back in his chair and breathes deep the sweet night air carrying in the scent of the trees and bushes outside his window, and he thinks of her as she always was, and smiles to himself to think that if she were alive now she would come in and put her hand through his hair and her arms around him and reproach him for letting the students tire him so; and he would confess to her that he'd been irritable with them for no apparent reason, and she would find an excuse for him and tell him that the students ought to be grateful anyway for receiving the attentions of such a good man. Many evenings after working like this in his study, and even more frequently of late, Burns rewards himself with thoughts of his dear wife, and never allows himself to consider his reveries an expression of loneliness.

Burns shaves his pencil and writes a conclusion to his notes, hand moving more slowly across the page now as exhaustion steals over him. Then a trace of a woman's perfume comes into the room, one he recognizes, and he's dimly aware of a presence behind him; and then a voice, sweet with loving care and lilting gently, like the point where song takes over from verse, but saying only what he so often hears now, always the same question which so lovingly framed commands the answer it seeks, "Isn't that enough work for tonight, L. P.?"

"Yes, my love," and he obediently puts down his pencil and returns his notebook to the top drawer of his desk.

Shadows thicken outside. Burns gets up and lowers the sash window, fastening the clasp at the top. On his way out he switches off the light. Talking to myself, he thinks with a brief smile, those kids will think me more senile than then they already do, and he closes the study door behind him.

TEN

Our dreams are a second life
—Gerard de Nerval

Then something astonishing happened. It was the morning of
their next scheduled meeting with Professor Burns. Near the waking moment, with the darkness peeling away, the flakes of light
stealing between blinds and through the partings in dreams, Lee
was lying asleep in his own room away from Ella, dreaming vividly
and with clear control. In the dream he looked down at his hands
and remembered, with absolute clarity, the appointment. There was
a whisper from somewhere, a message: *Do it.*

With ease he dissolved his surroundings and found himself in
the park, standing by the cherry tree close to the tennis courts
where he and Ella had had their first sexual encounter. The place
was absolutely still, cocooned in the grey light of a false dawn. A
mist hung around like wisps of cotton, as if trailed by a wind. The
air seemed unbearably tense. Lee could feel, physically feel, the
dawn about to crack, to split the light and open up a terrible, joyous
new day.

He waited. He had no sense of impatience. In the distance, taking shape through the mist, or perhaps just from the mist at the end
of the path, he could see someone walking towards him. It was not

Ella but Honora. She seemed somehow uncertain, hesitant. Then, as she got nearer, he realized he was mistaken. It was not Honora after all, but Ella. Ella had found her way to him! They were going to meet.

When Ella reached him, she smiled and stretched out a hand to touch his cheek; she was not shadow, nor phantom, but flesh and blood, warm and vital. He could feel the palm of her hand against the coolness of his cheek. He was gripped by a rage of excitement; he wanted to embrace her and shout. But at the same time he was caught in a kind of paralysis that inhibited and slowed his every move. His limbs were locked, his muscles contracted, the air around him congealed and thick, inhibiting movement and constraining all action, though his brain raced and his skin crawled, and a fist squeezed inside his belly. He wanted to shout, This is it! We did it! This is the meeting! But something happened to the breath that contained his words, and instead, in a voice that hardly seemed his own, he said:

There are more things in heaven and earth
than are dreamt of in your philosophy.

Ella smiled back at him, wordlessly, unmoving. They stood like that for some time, without discomfort, and then the dream dissolved.

Lee woke with a dull headache but with the dream clear in his mind. Shivering with excitement he pulled on his clothes and ran the full distance to Ella's house. Before hammering on the door, he leaned against the wall, panting heavily, trying to recover his breath, still shaking with anticipation; praying that Ella would confirm that the rendezvous had taken place and yet terrified that she would prove that all he had experienced was delusion cupped in a dream. He found the front door of the house ajar, and went through to Ella's room.

Inside he found Ella already dressed, sitting cross-legged on her mattress bed and writing in a book. She got up.

"I left the front door open for you."

"So," said Lee, "you were expecting me."

"There are more things in heaven and earth . . ."

Lee released a triumphant roar and took hold of Ella, the two of them dancing around the room in an ecstatic jig. He ran out into the yard, leaping and punching the air like a Cup Final goal scorer, then returned to Ella for further acclaim.

"You summoned me!"

"I did?" said Ella.

"You called me; it was your doing! I heard you. You did it!"

"I did? Really?" Ella allowed herself to be persuaded.

"Think hard," said Burns, "what was it, Honora, that you saw that made you lose the picture?"

Honora held her hands to her mouth, palms pressed together like someone in prayer. "I was on my way to the meeting place. I saw the path and the tennis courts; and then, by the cherry trees, I saw someone waiting. I remember thinking it might have been Lee, but I wasn't sure. Then I lost my way. That's all I can say. I lost my way."

"So when I thought I had mistaken Ella for Honora, it could actually have been Honora on her way to the rendezvous?" said Lee.

"It's possible; but it's not what I'm getting at. There is some block for Honora that made her 'lose her way' as she put it; otherwise she was clearly on the path to meeting up with you and Ella."

"We could try guided re-entry," suggested Brad.

"No," said Burns. "I don't want to surface any more of this material just yet. We may run the risk of disturbing a delicate process of development in dream control. My instincts tell me to let it incubate. Ella, tell us again how it felt for you." He leaned forward, eagerly.

"I had *the know*, in the way we've talked about before, the dreamside way of knowing. That sense which is more than a belief, it is a confident knowing that such-and-such is so, and in that way I knew that Lee would be waiting. There was no question about it. I didn't pause to think of Honora or Brad. The feeling of excitement was overwhelming. It was elation and anxiety mixed: that's what it was, that's what caused the kind of paralysis we both felt." Lee was nodding vigorously. "It was sexual too; we've discussed it and we both felt almost like the moment before orgasm. The tiniest mundane things were incredibly stimulating, and exciting things were unbearably so. That's why we hardly did anything, we were paralyzed by this feeling. When I touched Lee's face it was the most I could do; I mean the most. That's why, when he started quoting Shakespeare I thought it the most clever, profound and appropriate thing that could possibly have been said at that moment—less so now but at the time it was overwhelming!"

"But like I said, I didn't seem to have anything to do with it," said Lee, "and I wasn't trying to be clever. I went to say something like 'hallo Ella' and the other stuff is what came out."

"But what was remarkable," Burns observed, "is that not only did you meet, as previously agreed, but you also passed on a gift, a token, a message which you then brought into the objective reality of waking life. Do you realize what you've done? You've punctured a tiny hole in the membrane that separates the dream world from the waking one. Now we have to keep that hole open, and get Honora and Brad involved.

"Now; why that choice of place? Did it have resonance for Lee and Ella, but not for Brad and Honora? What we have to do now is find a tree where all four of you can, as it were, scratch your initials. I'll give the matter some thought. Meanwhile, see if the experience can be repeated. It should be possible to do something to overcome the paralysis you describe. The potential to think and move and act on dreamside, just as you would here, must ultimately be available to you. Brad and Honora—you must familiarize yourself with this particular spot in the park. At the moment that's all I can suggest. We may be moving towards a point where I can no longer give you advice. After all, you four are the practitioners, and my few theories are quickly being left behind. All I can do now is offer you an objective critique of the experiences you describe, evaluation at a distance.

"Now I'm feeling tired. Shall we call it a very big day?"

With the four of them gone, Burns sits hunched over his study desk, his window open to the thickening dark and the smells of moon-washed grass and earth. His Anglepoise lamp throws the disc of light around the paper on his desk and illuminates his skeletal hand scuttling back and forth. The pencil whispers to the page as it delivers its looping longhand scrawl, whispering, whispering as it goes, stopping only occasionally, like a creature listening for prey or predator; until the scuttling hand moves back in action to effect the compulsive writing of the old academic who fears he might have found more to say than he has time in which to say it.

ELEVEN

Traveller repose and dream among my leaves
—William Blake

Ella was waiting under the tree, a silhouette. From the distance Lee recognized the slope of her shoulder and the fall of her hair. In the next instant he was beside her, and she was smiling. He thought her eyes were like jewels, and then they were jewels—twin sapphires—and then they were eyes again. Ella touched him and he shivered. Touching almost broke the dream.

Then Ella was sitting in the tree. She was the tree spirit again. She blinked at him and he was sitting on the branch beside her.

—Did you make me do that? Or did I?—

—Do what?—

On dreamside, communication existed in a zone between thought and speech. You had spoken before you realized it. You thought after you had spoken. All communication seemed wide open to ambiguity and interpretation. Meanings generated new meanings.

—Make me be here. In the tree—

—In the tree?—

The muddle of the dreamspeak made them laugh. "In the tree" became for them an expression to explain the euphoric but confused, dithering condition of their dreaming state.

—Why all this mist?—It was a cobweb sheen, deadening all sound, filtering light through a grey sky, soaking the grass with heavy dew.

—Why all this mystery?—

—In the mist tree?—

They were drunk on dreaming.

—It's us! Us! See, Ella? We've fogged it. The mist. Tree. It's our own . . . dreamscape!—

—Can we change it?—

—Let's get rid of this mist and bring a sun up. Think it. Over there—He pointed to the eastern horizon. Ella focused.

And together they made the sun rise. Dreamside dawn was shell-pink and grey.

—Bigger—said Ella. The sun swelled visibly.

—More—The sun inflated again. It filled the sky, unnatural in its dimensions and pulsating with light. All mist had evaporated. The dew on the grass had dried.

—Change color—said Lee. The huge, throbbing disc changed from pink, to blood red, to tangerine, to liquid gold.

Ella gasped.—It's incredible. I feel like a painter! I feel like . . . —

—Like . . . God—

And so they walked together under the huge sun they had wrought. It was a world still moist from creation. They were afraid to touch each other.

—Lee. I love you Lee—

—I love you Ella—

The dream had a skin, a thin film which threatened to puncture at any moment. It also had a pulse, more sensed than heard, that kept time with their beating hearts and the throbbing energy of the sun. But this other pulse was frightening. They knew that when it stopped the dream would split at the seams.

—Do you feel it?—

—Yes. Like something trying to get in—

—It's frightening. Kiss me, Lee—

Lee turned to Ella. The idea of kissing her was more than he could bear. Even as he touched her, he felt the tiny hairline cracks appearing in the very fabric of the dream, and multiplying at astonishing speed.

Then suddenly, the dream broke.

The couple woke, shivering and exhausted.

Further dreamside encounters took place, characterized by that same intensity but always inhibited by an erratic sense of control. Lee and Ella reported that the paralysis which had gripped them on the first occasion had loosened and had opened up possibilities for further interaction, but that they still sometimes felt like live figures trapped in a painting. Any strenuous effort to act in a prescribed manner ran the risk of breaking up the dream. But progress was made and every small step was minutely observed and fêted by the group. They became insular and secretive, conspiratorial even, as their interest in the experience grew and their excitement increased.

Burns was becoming more than a little concerned that Brad and Honora were still unable to make the dream rendezvous, and that they were beginning to feel left behind, despite their encouragement and support for the successes of the other two. Even Brad had become less flippant, even a touch introspective as he struggled to catch up with the action. Both his and Honora's lucid dream control had progressed astoundingly, spurred on by the inspiration of their codreamers. But they repeatedly failed to find a path to the meeting place.

"It's like it's a closed place on dreamside," Brad complained, "anywhere else I can get to without a ticket. Sometimes I feel like I could shift to the Bank of England or to the Kremlin, but this place, somehow it never feels on."

Honora agreed. "I get a *know* about it. It's not an option, it's not on, I have the *know*."

Burns had come to trust the strength of the *dreamknow* to which Honora referred, and which only he of the five could not claim to have experienced. This *know* was more comprehensive, more fundamental than one's understanding in ordinary waking time, and he respected it deeply.

"Is it a fear, an anxiety or something that keeps you from the place where Ella and Lee meet?"

"I don't know. For us it's a neutral; a dead force field; a zone of used possibilities."

"Then we must find another zone or field."

"I had a fear," said Ella, "of someone else getting *in*."

"Oh?"

"L. P., can I ask you something?" Ella chancing the familiar mode while Burns was in a good mood.

"Ask away, E. I."

"Why are you so anxious to make all four of us rendezvous?"

"Is it a private party?"

"No; it's not that. I get the feeling you want further confirmation of what's happening."

"She means don't you trust us," said Lee.

"Yes Lee; I know what Ella means. But why shouldn't I trust your accounts?"

"We misled you at the beginning of the exercises. You would be right to be skeptical."

"Skeptical of you two I am not. Perhaps you will forgive my guard against credulity however, which springs from years of working in a discipline which has never been more than an Art which believes itself to be a Science. Even so, our capacity for self-deception and the unfaltering pursuit of wishful thinking are probably the most dependable of human attributes."

"So you do think we're making it all up!"

"Not so. Certainly not consciously, as in telling fibs to deceive a gullible old academic with nothing better to entertain him. No. But there is such a thing, to name an example, as a *folie à deux*."

"Madness between two emotionally involved people," said Brad cheerfully. "Where one feeds off the other's delusions."

"So we're liars or we're mad!"

"I'm not saying you're either of those, Ella, please don't make such a grim face at me. I'm pointing out that there are possibilities of illusory states of mind. Even with or without my spectacles I know you and Lee to be emotionally entangled. We have to consider these things. Now, a third or fourth party entering the scenario would help to confirm things."

"So if a second person sees the unicorn in the woods, it still doesn't exist," said Lee, "but if a third person sees it we'll give it a scientific name!"

"Speaking as someone who is a great believer in unicorns, I'd still want all three of them to have their heads tested!"

They all seemed to laugh longer at this quip than was necessary. The professor concluded the session. "Let's just say that it's much harder for three to keep up a conspiracy of self-deception than it is for two." Whatever that meant, they accepted it in good faith.

Three days later they called around at the professor's house and found him in high spirits. Still breaking open bottles left over from the end of term soirée, he announced his plans.

"It's time for us to find that tree I mentioned."

"What tree?"

"The one for you all to carve your initials on. By which I mean to say we now need to identify a new location as our point of rendezvous, one with which all four of you can have good strong associations, and which can become a new focus for us on dreamside. We are all going on a little summer holiday."

"Yay! When?"

"Tomorrow. Why not? Tomorrow is Midsummer Day. The weather is better than we deserve, and I know a rather beautiful spot where we can spend two or three days relaxing."

"Relaxing! Yo! Where is it?"

"Wait and see. The idea is for us to spend some time there, relax, soak up the beautiful countryside, grow even closer as a group, make associations with the place, absorb some of its nature . . . Are you persuaded?"

"We're persuaded! Let's do it!"

Next morning they travelled southwards, squeezed into the professor's cherished Morris Minor, Burns driving slowly and with exasperating caution. The sun got up hot overhead, bouncing off the polish and chrome of the car and cooking its passengers. The girls' bare legs stuck to the leather upholstery and Lee and Brad both took off their shirts, sitting bare chested and sweating. Burns, dressed in collar and tie, sweater and tweed suit, steered carefully with hands gripped permanently at five-minutes-to-one, resisting all overtures either to drive faster or to reveal their destination.

In Coventry he turned sharply into a one-way street and a flow of oncoming traffic. A policeman stuck his head out of his car window and bellowed at him to pull over. Particulars were noted and Burns, who remained calm and polite throughout, was instructed to produce his driving documents at a police station within fourteen days.

"An unfortunate development," he muttered when they were mobile again.

"It's nothing," said Brad, "all you have to do is take in your licence and insurance and stuff."

"I don't have one. A driving license I mean."

"What!"

"Nor any of the other documents he mentioned. Insurance and such."

"Eh!"

"I only take the car out once or twice a year, around the block as it were, just to keep it going. I resent having to insure it for that. Is it likely that they will make a fuss, do you think?"

"Just keep going," someone said, "we'll try not to think about it."

"Right; fuck the pigs!" screamed Ella through the open window, and with such revolutionary ardor that Burns was startled, or possibly inspired, into driving marginally faster for the rest of the journey.

They reached the Brecon hills around lunchtime, and Burns drove them to an isolated house, belonging, he said, to a colleague. The place was rudimentary, some kind of holiday cottage equipped in utilitarian fashion. They ran up and down the stairs quickly claiming rooms, Ella and Lee together, Honora alone and Brad accepting a camp bed arrangement with good grace so that L. P. didn't have to scramble with the rest of them to stake out his territory in the front bedroom of the house. The old professor looked utterly exhausted by the journey, and sank down into a chair. When someone shouted that neither shower nor bath was functioning, he looked apologetic and bewildered, and could only suggest that they bathe in a lake he knew of, some three or four miles down the road.

Ella could see how tired he was. She went over to him. "It doesn't matter about the bath. It would be great fun to swim in the lake. And the house and the countryside are wonderful." He looked reassured by her words and forced a brief smile. The others realized that they were going to have to slow down over the next few days unless they wanted an invalid on their hands.

They took him at his word about the lake, and Brad persuaded him (by dint of hard work and outrageous promises) to surrender the car keys for the drive down to it. Again they all squeezed into the uninsured Morris Minor together with a deckchair for Burns to sit on while they swam. Burns complained that they were treating him like a geriatric, but was obviously gratified by this consideration.

The lake was cool and inviting. They parked the car at the side of the road and walked down to its grassy banks. An ancient oak leaned out over it, root and branch plunging into the dark, deep water. They made camp under a row of weeping willows which dipped leafy stems into the blueblack cool. A spiral of excited swallows wheeled and turned and dotted the sky with parabolas above the lake, intoxicated by their own matchless aerial display.

Burns's deckchair was set up with protracted ceremony and discussion. Only when he was fully installed did the others undress and leap squealing into the water. He watched them swim and bob, and laid towels out on the grass for them. Then he returned to his deckchair, where he promptly fell into a doze.

It must have been two hours before he woke. The sun had slipped in the sky. Everything slumbered. Something of the lake's calm had distilled itself into the afternoon tranquillity. Glancing down, he saw four young bodies basking in the heat, their smiling faces lifted up to him as if they expected him to speak.

"Did you dream lucid dreams L. P.?" Lee asked lazily.

Honora said, "You were talking in your sleep."

Ella giggled. "We heard everything. You named names."

"Lilly? Did I say Lilly?"

"Yes."

Burns smiled sleepily and settled back in his chair. "Lilly was my wife. You know, she died more than ten years ago. I've been dreaming of her a lot lately. Good dreams, nice dreams. We used to come here, often, years and years ago. Beautiful, peaceful; just as it is now. It hasn't changed at all. That's why I thought of this place."

"I love it," said Honora.

"We can have some pleasant days here before returning. There should be a rowing boat in the shed. We can bring it down here, or rather you can. There's fishing tackle if you're interested. Or we can take a walk through the woods there." They all agreed that the choice had been fine—quiet, unspoiled, entirely tranquil.

The next three days were a summer idyll. The weather held

out, and time seemed suspended as they swam in the lake, picnicked under the spreading oak, drifted in the rowing boat, or went on long walks in the cool fern woods. Burns in particular loved to stroll in the woods, along narrow pathways winding between giant ferns, with the echoing rap of an unseen woodpecker as descant to his students' conversation. He liked to stroll with each of them in turn, probing, challenging, teasing them with his gentle irony.

They would return from these walks shaking their heads at the breadth of his knowledge, waiting for him to fall asleep in his deckchair before relaying an impression of their discussions to the others. It seemed that he could talk with authority about anything, pick up their own arguments and generously advance them before dismantling them with an opposing view. Lee found him fascinating on the psychosexual meaning of fairy-tales, of all things, and stalked the woods discussing the sexual imagery of Beauty and the Beast; Ella could listen all day to his analysis of revolutionary history or to his satirical monologue on the psychology of the fascist disposition; Honora found him an expert on Surrealism; and Brad had his eyes opened on everything from football to the pharmaceutical industry. Though they never did see a unicorn in those dense, aromatic woods, the possibility of doing so had never seemed so close.

Burns was generally content to sit quietly in his deckchair, watching events take their predictable shape. There was little in the splashing and cavorting of the four young students to make this grey-haired scholar of human behavior raise an eyebrow, but he saw—where they might not—the doomed infatuation of Lee and Ella, too hot not to burn itself out too soon; Brad's persistent and not unsubtle advances on Honora, gently but firmly deflected; Brad's disguised interest in Ella, secretly recognized and shrugged off by her but completely missed by Lee; and the subtle affection Lee and Honora reserved for each other, prompting more speculation by others than it ever did for them.

And while he watched all this with fond interest, it added to, rather than detracted from, the uninhibited delight of three perfect summer days. How could it be otherwise, when the place itself was a kind of dream? But beyond that which he would always see with his trained eye, he could never have guessed at, nor would he ever have permitted, the growth of those strange forms already tightening round that close circle of four, like snaring vines in a wood, or like dangerous weeds reaching from the bedrock of a lake to the thrashing ankles of careless swimmers.

TWELVE

And I too in Arcadia
—Anon

In the following weeks, the group made five almost effortless rendezvous experiments on dreamside. The dreamside location, the site of their recent summer trip, was easily called to mind during bouts of ordinary dreaming. Appointments were made and were kept.

Burns resisted their impatience to return and return again to dreamside, so hot was their excitement, and insisted that the rendezvous took place no more frequently than once per week so as not to fatigue their powers or jade the sharpness of the experience. For him it was a time of furious notetaking and exhaustive post-dream analysis, questioning the four ever more assiduously, pressing more closely in his collection of minutiae for the construction of a theory that held little interest for them. Their direct experience was like bathing in incandescent light, while the professor wanted to grope in the shadows. He became at times irascible, frustrated at their inability to crystallize the unbearable excitement of the elusive, drifting experience of their dreamside rendezvous.

"To be there is to know," Lee tried lamely during one post-dream analysis, "and to know is to be there."

Burns threw down his notepad and pencil. "So, Lee, you've had a few nice dreams and now you're a Zen Master." He leaned forward, a crimson rash spreading over his forehead as he spat the words, an iron-grey lock of hair loosening and lashing at his face. "Look; God or nature equipped you with the most accurate and poetic language in the history of nations. You have at your disposal the precision of the Latin and the expressiveness of the Germanic, and you were born lucky enough to ride the confluence of both. Why don't you use it because I DON'T HAVE THE FUCKING TIME FOR YOUR MORONIC BABBLING UNDERGRADU-ATE BUDDHIST LAMENT."

They were shocked into silence. Burns had obviously learned how to swear. He looked ill.

"Forgive me, I'm raving," he said at last, "I do apologize."

"No," said Lee, "I was being sloppy; you're right. Let's start again."

"Maybe a short break for coffee?" Ella suggested.

It was during this break that Honora complained of something peculiar which had happened to her that morning. "I woke up, washed and dressed, went out of the door and—"

"You woke up," said Brad.

"You had it too?"

"Couple of times."

"More than a couple," said Ella.

All four of them had experienced what they called "false awakenings," dreams of waking up which were so prosaic that they could not be distinguished from the actual experience of waking into the real world. Lee testified that he had even experienced the false awakening twice in the same morning.

"It can get so you don't know if you've woken or you haven't."

"Or whether you are just about to," Ella put in.

"An interesting side effect," said Burns. The others weren't so sure how interesting it was.

———

Their dreamwork analysis continued. They could easily describe how they had managed to rendezvous on dreamside, how they had touched or talked or even how they had once swum together. But these adventures held no particular fascination for Burns. He was far more interested in the fact that on dreamside most of the events took place without words: if there was an agreement to swim, they simply dived in, it was understood, and if there was an idea to move off in one direction together then it was communicated at some mysterious subverbal level. Burns set them the exercise of passing on messages during dreamtime, usually slogans or proverbs or short quotations. Such a task required considerable discipline. Words would sometimes come, but as with Lee's original breakthrough, not always the intended message. Results were mixed and communication was unstable. Burns became more demanding.

At last, another breakthrough was made. It did become possible to stabilize the dreamside scenario and deliver the appropriate message which was then generally recalled upon awakening, but this required tremendous efforts of concentration on both the part of the giver and the receiver, quite often with the result that the weight of concentration would itself break up the dream. This difficulty notwithstanding, the four became increasingly proficient at stabilizing the flow of the dream and passing on or picking up the words which had been selected for them by the professor.

There was one drawback. This developing skill was accompanied by an increase in frequency of the false awakenings. It was not uncommon for three or four such unpleasant and disturbing experiences to be stacked one on top of the other. Another word of special significance crept into the dreamer's argot: *the repeater*.

Burns persisted with his interest in information transmission, so rigorously that they began to joke that he was working for the intelligence services, or perhaps for some foreign power. Burns took this in good part, camping it up and telling them that they would never know, would they, but he was not to be deflected from his purposes. Then he suggested that one of them might take a book, any book, to dreamside, and attempt to read it.

The task was beyond their capacity. But, although it proved a failure, it failed spectacularly, yielding some interesting information for Burns, and generating further passionate scribbling.

To begin with, no one could ever "remember" to transport a book to dreamside. Though they planned it conscientiously enough, even selecting a particular work by a favorite author and placing it by their bedsides, the task never occurred to them until they had returned from dreamside and awakened to see the volume lying nearby. After several failures of this kind they told Burns that they thought the books had been too "heavy" to "carry," and Burns said he thought he knew what they meant by that.

Then, after the task had been dropped, Brad arrived on dreamside holding a book, though, disappointingly, it turned out not to be a book that he had ever chosen to bring with him. Brad and Lee inspected it together. They opened the pages at random and read:

> I dreamt that I dwelt in marble halls
> With vassals and serfs at my side,
> And of all who assembled within these walls
> That I was the hope and the pride

Neither of them recognized the verse, but when they looked at the lines again a few moments later, those very same lines had changed, now reading very differently:

> I dreamt I dwelt in marble halls
> Where each damp thing that creeps and crawls
> Went wobble-wobble on the walls.

The transformation produced much hilarity. But when they looked back to check the lines a third time, they were changed yet again:

> *I'll dreamt that I'll dwealth mid warblers' walls*
> *when throstles and choughs to my sigh hiehied.*

This metamorphosis of the words went on endlessly. All they had to do was look away, and then look back at the page, for the words to undergo another completely new transformation.

When they reported this to Burns, they were unable to recall any of the words at all, only that they changed continually. Burns was fascinated, but ultimately concluded that the effort was wasted and that the exercise with the books could stop.

"It's disconcerting," Brad was saying, "you don't know whether to bother to wash your face in the morning in case you have to do it again." The *repeaters* were beginning to disturb them.

"Sometimes it's not pleasant," Honora agreed. "You can spend a whole day thinking that you might be going to wake up any time. You only feel sure when you put your head down to go to sleep again, and even then you're not so sure; you know: dreams within dreams."

Burns became concerned. "All I can suggest is that you use some signal demonstrably external to your dream to wake you, a telephone call or more practically an alarm clock which you set at different times each night so that you are jolted out of your dream. Beyond that perhaps you should try to enjoy, and live to the full, your other new 'lives'."

"Thanks," said Brad.

Of course, it was possible to dream of being awakened by an alarm clock in repeaters, but in general the professor's advice was useful, and although the repeaters did not abate, the experience of them became less sinister. Then Burns recalled the failed exercise in reading. He reminded them of the instability of written information on dreamside, and suggested that they might turn to printed material as an acid test of whether or not they were awake. If they read a line or two from a book, then reread it to find that it remained constant, they could assume to have awakened. They found this practice successful, and adopted it as a critical test. Somehow the test eluded them when actually inside the repeaters, but it was easy to remember when awake. It was felt to be an encouraging remedy, and so kept much of the anxiety about repeaters at bay.

Term time came around and students returned *en masse* to the university. For Honora, Lee and Ella this was to be their final year. On the first day of the new term Ella called around at the professor's house to deliver her dreamwork notes. The door was answered by his cleaning lady, who told Ella that the professor had been taken to hospital and was in the coronary unit.

Burns was sat up in bed, propped by a mound of pillows, smiling faintly.

"How did I know you would come?"

"Has no one else been?" asked Ella.

Burns shrugged. "I just hoped one of you would come."

"They told me I could only see you for a few minutes. The others will come when they hear that you've been brought in like this. Is there someone to get things for you? I mean I know there isn't, what I'm saying is, can I get anything . . . ?"

Burns seemed to have barely enough strength to turn his head. He opened and closed his mouth but no words came out. Then he beckoned her to come closer, and as she leaned forward he grasped her wrist with surprising force. He spoke in a hoarse whisper. "I was dreaming. Dreaming of Lilly. My wife, you remember I told you about her that day by the lake? My lovely wife. You were teasing me, remember? Lilly."

"Yes, I remember you telling us about her."

"Listen to me. I was dreaming of Lilly. She kissed me and she gave me a telling-off. She said I was to leave you young people alone."

Ella shook her head. She was a little frightened by his intensity.

"Listen, Ella. I'm very happy with what we achieved but I would like the dreaming to stop now. Lilly's right, as usual. She's right. I want you to tell the others that it has gone far enough and that now it should stop." He let go of her wrist, his own hand falling onto the bed.

"I don't understand, Professor. Is there anything wrong with what we do?"

"Just understand that I don't want you to continue."

"We wouldn't unless you wanted us to."

"That's right. Now I'd like to sleep."

"I'll come tomorrow." But she wasn't sure if he was already asleep.

Ella returned to the campus and to Lee's room. They climbed into bed, talking about Burns. At some time during the dark hours close to morning Ella dreamed—and knew that she was dreaming—that Burns came through the door of their room. His right arm was stretched out towards her, his palm open, and he said:

He hath awakened from the dream of life.

In the morning Ella phoned the hospital, and an anonymous voice confirmed what she already knew.

THIRTEEN

I can never decide whether my dreams are the
result of my thoughts, or my thoughts the result of
my dreams
—D. H. Lawrence

"I say we carry on," said Brad. The four had assembled in Lee's cell-sized room. Brad was peering into the mirror, where he seemed to have found something of enormous charm, and couldn't tear himself away.

"We've heard ten times what you say; we're trying to find out what others might think." Ella was perched on the one available chair looking at Honora, who sat on the bed with her knees drawn up under her chin. Lee lay on his back on the floor blowing smoke rings while balancing an ashtray on his stomach.

Brad continued to address his own reflection. "It's just beginning to get interesting. It will all have been for nothing if we quit now."

"I feel like I made a kind of promise to L. P.," said Ella.

"You shouldn't have."

"No, Brad, but I did. I'm not inclined to stop the dreamwork; it's the most exciting thing that's ever happened to me. But he got a bit spooky that night in the hospital. A kind of warning. He was really quite anxious."

"Lee thinks we should carry on," said Brad.

"Yup," said Lee.

"Is that all you've got to say?" Ella gave Lee a look intended to be intimidating.

"Yup."

"Honora?"

"I think we could continue. But we should be careful."

"Careful of what?"

"Just careful."

Brad turned from his reflection to face the others. "Let me just say this and it will be my last word on the matter."

"Wonderful," said Ella.

"Hear me out. You all saw how important this project was to L. P. It became a consuming interest for him, almost an obsession. We're involved in a major breakthrough in the field of parapsychology research: he knew it and we know it. L. P. was an academic and what do *they* want except to go down in academic history as being at the head of their field, even if it means exploiting a few talented students on the way . . . all right, all right," fending off a few weak protests from the others, "I liked the old boy as much as any of you, but what I'm saying is, he knew the absolute fucking *potential* of this thing.

"That's why his brief to us was to keep working on the passing of information; while we were caught up in the excitement and pleasure of what happens on dreamside he wanted information. If we were ever capable of controlling this message transmission . . . use your brains! . . . the telephone would be as obsolete as the carrier pigeon, governments would pay fortunes for knowledge of this ability, they'd pour millions into research, and what's more we would be indispensable. Know what I'm talking about?"

No one answered, so Brad continued. "Lee, Honora, what have you got in mind for your careers. Teaching? Selling? What about you Ella? Full time revolutionary? What I'm talking about could be a way of life."

"I got the point."

Lee stubbed out his cigarette and sat up. "I've got a proposal.

We continue with the experiments, but in a disciplined way. If any one of us becomes unhappy about the way things are going and wants to stop, then we stop, and what's more all four of us stop."

"Why?" said Brad. "Why should just one person be able to pull the plug on all the others?"

"I can't explain it properly, but you know—you *know!*—that there's something about this whole dreamwork enterprise that has a *corporate* feel to it. An entanglement. On dreamside if one person shivers, the others feel it. That means a special responsibility, so I say: One Out All Out."

Ella and Honora were nodding vigorously in agreement.

"OK," said Brad.

"No, not just OK. If we're doing it at all, we're doing it with a commitment."

Ella sighed. "There goes my promise to L. P."

"A deathbed promise," said Honora.

So they continued. Interest in their final-year studies was suspended as they attempted to make progress on dreamside with the same air of discipline with which the professor had moderated and controlled their earlier experiments. The dreamside rendezvous took place once a week, with clear objectives and exercises to be conducted in the dreamtime scenario of the lake, the over-arching oak tree and the adjacent woods. It was followed by rigorous recording and reporting and the assembly of copious notes. Post-dream meetings were discussed and analysed, and progress was monitored.

But without the detached observation and charismatically imposed discipline of Professor Burns, this academic rigor came to seem empty. Measured against the intensity of the dreamside experience, the four began to feel as though their notebooks were nothing more than a shrine to Burns's memory. The excitement of the

encounters had not blunted: they continued to experience everything as they had described it to the professor, shivering on the edge
of orgasm, on the brink of some overwhelming discovery which
would come—not yet, not quite yet, but which *was* there and which
would come.

And it was how it felt that mattered. Physically it felt like the
skin had been peeled back to expose nerves that sighed at every
breath of wind. The mere proximity or movement of others made
teasing waves in the air. Every pore ached with pleasure. Yet underneath this sensuous carnival lay something else. It was an anxiety, a
misgiving; one which they all felt but to which, curiously, they never
referred. This anxiety was always there, like an unpleasant taste in
the mouth, and grew in proportion to the level of excitement or
pleasure they experienced.

Ordinary and trivial details seemed exciting, and exciting
things were overwhelming. So, when Lee kissed Ella and put his
tongue into her mouth, the fabric of the dream broke, like a bubble
rising in the air and bursting soundlessly. And it broke not just for
Lee and Ella but unaccountably for Honora and Brad as well.

It was against this degree of intensity that the message-passing
experiments were conducted. Competing against the narcotic plea-
sures of exploring other dreamside powers, it became a dismal chore.
Without the influence of the professor, interest in these experiments
degenerated into a gamesy sequence of feats and tricks performed
only for amusement, such as Lee's discovery of how to disappear
behind the oak tree and reappear immediately somewhere else, like
an actor who could exit stage left and enter stage right. Then they
found the rowing boat drawn up against the shore as if they had
conveniently left it. Floating the boat on the water became an
absorbing pastime. When at first the touch of the boat on the skin of
the water had been enough to puncture and end the dream, it
became possible to float the small craft and to clamber into it, before
the dream burst. All of this was enchanting and bewildering, and

altogether more fun as the discipline of scientific observation was neglected.

Autumn term passed in a goldening and withering of leaves barely noticed by the four students, whose disdain of studies did not go unnoticed by university authorities. But written warnings only became certificates of bravado in the collective dreamwork enterprise. At Christmas that year they went home on shortened holidays, returning early to recommence the program of dreaming.

Then came a disruption to the scheduled program, introduced so naturally that if anyone was immediately aware of its irregularity they forgot to, or chose not to, comment on it. At least not until later. Somewhere between the strict pattern of the weekly rendezvous a second meeting quietly inserted itself and became established as if by tacit agreement. No such additional rendezvous had ever been discussed in waking time, yet the four arrived at that same lakeside location in no state of surprise, as if washed back there by cool currents or unnoticed tides. Then one unofficial rendezvous became two or three, or more, until any regular pattern or monitored schedule was lost.

The second disruption was of a more human order. Brad started to look upon Lee and Ella's amorous dreamside behavior with a dangerously jealous eye. Honora meanwhile was determinedly preserving from him the virginity she thought worth keeping. She had so far managed to resist Brad's playful and charmless advances as emphatically on dreamside as she did in waking time.

Brad's seduction line—delivered in the thinkspeak of dreamtime, a combination of thoughts and mouthed utterances into which millions of ambiguities and misunderstandings could seem to fly—failed to persuade her.—You're the luckiest girl ever to have lived—he murmured to her on one dreamside encounter—I mean have your cake and eat it won't you; have the beauty of knowing what it's like and still being a virgin, it doesn't count on dreamside—

—Oh yes?—

—Yeah!; there's no sin on dreamside—

—I don't know about that. Let's just take the boat on the lake instead—

Brad didn't regard that as much of an *instead*. At times he took to following Lee and Ella around, making a crowd of himself even in the vast space of dreamside. Lee and Ella got as tired of Brad's prurient interests on dreamside as they would have done in waking time. It wasn't simply a question of finding a quiet spot out in the woods somewhere, because space and distance didn't count the same. Brad was just a thought away if he wanted to be, and he often did, warm on their warmth, breathing on their breath. Until then neither a cross word nor an unkind thought had passed between them on dreamside, but Ella this time thoughtspelled it out for Brad.

—Can't you leave us alone we've got some private experiments to conduct which require the presence of two people only—

—Don't mind me. I'll make notes—

At which Ella turned and spoke to Brad. Not in the thinkspeak unique to dreamside, but in clear loud English as she successfully transmitted an old and unambiguous message: "FUCK OFF, COUSINS!"

Brad was deeply shocked, as was Lee, at the waves of hard energy that radiated from the violence of Ella's words. Ella too was surprised and held her hands at her mouth as if to stop anything else which might want to come out. The very air around them seemed appalled; but to their surprise the dream absorbed the dull explosion of Ella's words as if they were shells detonating against the membrane of its walls, leaving Brad to turn his back and cross some threshold which would dissolve it all for him anyway.

FOURTEEN

O God! I could be bounded in a nutshell
and count myself a king of infinite space—
were it not that I have bad dreams
—Shakespeare

Was it before Ella dreamcursed Brad Cousins, or was it some-time after his rupture of the dreamside idyll that events there took a dark turn?

"Something's not quite right about the place," Ella said to Honora about dreamside. "Not quite the same as the *real* place, the orig-inal place. Something I can't put my finger on."

"No birds for one."

Ella instantly knew that Honora was right. No birds for sure, try that out for size; and therefore no insects either to play on the mirror surface of the lake. But it wasn't only that, there was something in the substance, the resin of the place, under the surface of things. It was a constant presence, attendant and right in front of you, but which only became more elusive the more you tried to identify it.

What was it?

But no one could recall exactly when the first *elementals* started to take hold. One rendezvous ran into another with no sense of chronology to slice them apart, no sequence of night or day. There was only the dreamed sun that never burned, and all note-taking discipline had gone.

Now they were able to sustain and control the dreaming long

enough to feel tired by their efforts, knowing that their energies were sapped by the work of fixing and holding the dream in place. This fatigue always came as a signal that perhaps they had stayed too long this time, and in the form of a lapse in control of events, a confusion, a loss of purpose. Then, in one deep-dreaming fog, Honora laid her head back on the grass under the protection of that giant oak and closed her eyes.

Shaking her mass of nut-brown curls from under her she felt the touch of the warm grass and the exposed knots of tree root on her neck. She could feel the warmth of the fixed sun on her face. The lapping water spread a deep sense of calm, and she thought that even within sleep it might be possible to test for another sleep, dream within lucid dream.

The other three had moved off somewhere, faded into the periphery of the dream, her dream or their dream. In the peace around her she heard a drowsy whispering, a rustle like a breeze in the leaves of the trees but something more intimate, almost a murmuring coming from the lake or from the tree roots, but soothing, and whispering unrecognizable, comforting words. She relaxed, letting go completely. The air was scented with balm and she felt good about the warm grass and the exposed tree roots touching her white neck like the gently exploring fingertips of a lover's hands, then intertwining in the spilled ringlets of her long hair, stroking, winding into her hair, gently pulling her deeper into the grass, weaving her hair into the grass and the roots of the tree, pulling it downwards and into the black soil. It was easy just to go with it, let it play, let it take you down, become part of it, let it become part of you. Honora heard a tiny splash from the lake far off, and realized what was happening.

She had to swim her way back to consciousness. It was a fight. It felt as if she were actually struggling to pull her hair from the grass and the roots dragging her down. It became impossible to distinguish between the loom of hair, grass, root and soil, so perfect a woven fabric had they made in the natural carpet at the foot of the tree. Honora fought for breath in a rising panic, thrashing wildly, her heartbeat echoing aloud in the earth from which she tried to tear loose. At last she felt her hair snapping and her scalp searing as she wrenched herself upright, screaming, arms flailing, to find Brad, Lee and Ella all stooped over her.

—Was it a dream, a nightmare? I mean within this dream, did you close your eyes and sleep?—

Lee helped Honora to her feet. They could see wisps of her hair still entangled in the roots.

For a while the horror of it shook them, until they dismissed the event as some kind of nightmare taking place within the wheel of the dream. They were wrong. Their complacency was further shaken when Lee had a not dissimilar experience of his own.

Lee and Ella were out on the lake, drifting in the small boat, its keel not piercing the still skin of the water. While the excitement of being on dreamside never waned, the exhaustion of consciously sustaining the dream was closing in. They lay in the boat, fighting off the second sleep, the surrender that might take them back, Ella humming softly, Lee dipping a hand in the water over the side of the boat. The scene was lit by a pallid disk that could have been the moon but was the unshifting sun burning without energy. Lee sensed a low breathing from the trees or the water, or maybe from the gentle swell and fall of his own lungs. Maybe the secret was inside him, so easy was it to be at peace, to merge with the background, give up, yield and become fluid, like the stir of water between his fingers. A gradual loss of temperature permeated his hand, blood pulsed gently at his fingertips, his veins leaking, flesh and blood dissolving without pain and commingling with the lake water in a sweet seduction that could take everything.—NOOO!— Lee sat up in the rowing boat and screamed. His arm was paralyzed. He struggled to lift it from the water, his muscles refusing to unlock until, gasping with pure terror, he felt his arm release with a scorching pain and a sound like newspaper tearing.

—What is it? What happened?—Lee's scream had caught Ella mid-song, and now she sat up in the boat taking Lee's head in her hands.

—I don't know I don't know—Lee looked in horror over the side of the boat at the thin eel-like trails of blood already diffusing into the blue-black water.—I want to get out—

There the dream broke.

They all experienced it in different ways. For Brad it began with a perspiration that grew into a sweat which threatened a melting as if he was made of plastic; for Ella the earth, seeming to want to become part of her, reconstituted her feet as the warm soil.

These lucid nightmares were more terrifying than anything in ordinary dreaming: for what might happen if the absorbing process continued to its conclusion? The implications for waking time were not to be contemplated. So, they guarded themselves. Their dreaming became circumspect, as they proceeded in fear of another attack.

It was Brad who showed them how to deal with these *elementals*. He called them together on dreamside.

—Watch—he said, bringing them over to the trunk of the oak, and pressing the palm of his hand against its rough bark. He closed his eyes as they watched. At first nothing happened. Then his fingernails slowly took on a glaucous color, changing slowly to moss-green, which moved imperceptibly down his fingers until the lines and folds and knuckles of his hand deepened and cracked, and his fingernails split. Then his hand absorbed the texture of solid bark spreading across the back of his hand to his wrist, his fingertips transforming into a stunted branch of the tree itself: gnarled, knotted, living tree:

— Stop it—Honora whispered.

—Not yet—The creeping bark inched up his arm, cracking and resetting his bones as it went, twisting at a point below his elbow.

—Stop it!—

—Now!—said Brad, and the metamorphosis stopped dead. His hand was organically joined with the trunk; the rough bark texture of his limb indistinguishable from the bark of the tree. But the process had been halted.

—You've become sloppy! Forgotten the art of lucid dreaming!—said Brad with contempt.—There's no time here, you just have to think it back, reverse the process, think it back, just like rewinding a film. Watch—

The growth which had taken possession of Brad's limb retreated exactly as it had advanced, moving back down the arm and across the hand like a long glove being peeled off, the rough texture dissolving, the moss-green tincture vanishing until his hand reformed itself entirely.

Brad held up his unscathed hand for all of them to see.—Learn it—he said.

FIFTEEN

There is no law to judge of the lawless,
or canon by which a dream may be criticized
—Charles Lamb

Harmony and security were restored to dreamside, at least for a while. Brad had demonstrated, and the others were able to reproduce, the powers that would keep the frightening encroachment of those elemental forces at bay. Lee and Ella were free to persist with their "orgasm project": the sexual adventure of making it happen on dreamside. But they had difficulty with sustaining the dream long enough to contain such a high pitch of excitement. The dream always seemed to crack at a crucial moment.

This left Brad to look on, and Honora to resist. It wasn't long before Brad decided that just *being* on dreamside wasn't enough.

—Know what they're doing, Honora?—

—Of course. Enjoying it, I hope—

—Doesn't it make you curious?—

—About them? No—

—No, not about them. I mean about it. *It*. It must be different here. Incredible. Different. The end of the world—

—I wouldn't know—

—No, you wouldn't would you? Maybe you should watch them, find out how it's done—

—I don't think they'd like to be watched; any more than I would—

—C'mon. There's just you and me here—

—Perceptive—

—Know what? I want you badly—

—Don't start—

—Don't start? It never stops! What am I supposed to do? What about me?—

—Poor Brad; he isn't getting any—

They had rehearsed this discussion before, both on dreamside and in waking time.

—Am I so obnoxious?—

—I prefer you as a friend—

—I hate people who say that—

—So if you hate me you can't want me—

Uninterested as she was, Honora knew anyway that Brad's real feelings were for Ella. She could see what Ella would have dismissed out of hand; what Lee preferred not to see; and what Brad could never admit. Yet there was no question. Brad was secretly in love with Ella, and because he had no chance of getting close he made a mask of perpetual antagonism towards her. He was the only one suffering from this conspiracy to deny the obvious.

Honora felt some sympathy for him, if only because she alone could see what was burning him up. Brad could only vent his feelings destructively. When Ella was around, he would mock or goad or challenge her in ways which at least won some form of contact, even if it was negative. He drew strength from the friction. And when Ella disappeared with Lee, he paced around Honora in a froth of agitation. He was a danger to himself.

—Honora, think of what you could be missing!—

—I thought of it—

—And?—

—I'll pass—

—It's an experience denied to other people! It's like being specially chosen for something! It's one of life's great miracles and it's only available to us! Don't throw it away!—

—Still, I'll pass—

—You're a stupid naïve silly little country virgin who doesn't know anything—

—Oh I'm not so naïve; all the other things maybe—

She got up and moved away from Brad's hot attention, leaning her back against the oak tree. She thought of Lee and Ella, briefly, naked in the long grass.

—I'm not that naïve—she said again.

For Lee and Ella were only a thought away, stretched amid the daisies and the long grass, shivering at each other's hot breath and warm touch. It was as if they had cast off not just their clothes but also their living skin, leaving them a bundle of exposed nerve endings, detonating at every breath of air, kiss, or light caress. Achingly sensitive to subtle changes in the air currents around them, Ella leaned across Lee and pressed her tongue on his stiffened penis, flicking at the dome with her tongue, *here is the church*, her lips settling and lifting and resettling on him like a butterfly's beating wings, *here is the steeple*, Lee in an agony of tumescence, the unstoppable swelling, the ecstatic unknowable voice in his ears until he thought the whole thing would explode, not just his cock but his brain, his head, his body, the dream, life outside the dream, life beyond that, until Ella brought him sharply back under control, coaxing and reminding him to hold it together.

—Slow it—she said.—Slow. Breathe deep. Imagine I've got a knife at your throat and I'm making you do this, now do it, put it inside me—

—Prove it—said Brad.

—What?—said Honora.

—Prove that you're not. Not naïve—

Brad stood up. His gaze locked on her and she felt unable to look away, mesmerized, as if he were holding her head so that she couldn't turn away. The air around was absolutely still, not a whisper of wind in the air, but she felt a strange shift in the currents, something akin to a breeze lift gently at the nut-brown curls nestling on her neck. Although he stood fully ten feet away, she knew it was some force that Brad was exerting.

—What are you doing?—

—Prove it to me—Brad said again.

—Don't—said Honora, unable to take her eyes from his.

Brad didn't take a single step closer, but he continued to fix her with his gaze. She was unable to move. She felt the silver buckle of the patent leather belt around her skirt open, the belt passing itself through the loops of her skirt, moving off her like a live thing, like a snake which dropped at her feet. Then she felt a button of her blouse gently popping open above her breasts, followed by the next, and the next down to her waist, and the blouse being lifted back from her shoulders exposing her breasts to him.

—Don't—Honora said again, her arms fallen at her side, held down by a strange paralysis, not knowing how to resist, wanting to fight back and reverse what was happening, think it back as with the elementals, but not finding the strength.

—You can stop it any time you want—he said.

—God, I just can't move! Don't you see I don't want this?—

—Any time you want—

Was he right? Could she stop it? She tried, but couldn't. There was nothing she could do. Then she felt the button go at the side of her skirt and heard the toothrasp of the zip opening, and the skirt fell around her legs, lying in a hoop at her feet. At last she felt the elastic of her panties being rolled down her thighs and falling to her feet.

Brad stepped forward.

Control. Lee fought for control, imagining that Ella's sharp fingernails on his throat were indeed a knife, until in the dream it was the
gleaming blade she would plunge into his neck if he failed to please
her; *open the door*, I love you for ever, he pushed inside her and she
squeezed him to her, laying her head back on the grass. It was unbearable this dreamside sex, like making love on a live cable of electric
wire. Stay with it, she was whispering, stay with it, but he knew it
would have to finish or stop or the dream must break. He was clench-
ing handfuls of her hair in his fists and the grass and daisies growing
at the side of her head were mixed up in her hair, and she became a
human shape of glittering white-hot energy, pulsating and glittering
and burning. He felt they were making love astride a howling wind
and over a rushing current and then when he felt her coming he gave
in to the current and the wind and felt his body spurting light from
every pore of his body as the dream imploded and was over.

The next morning Lee woke up next to Ella, feeling strange, dislocated and energized. She was still sleeping. He kissed her, and in her
hair he found a daisy head, two daisy heads, and torn blades of grass.
He woke Ella to show them to her.

Grass and daisy heads on the pillow: evidence in the day's eye of
what had been transported from dreamside.

Honora Brennan woke up alone in her bed and pushed back the
bedcovers to inspect the speckled crimson stains on the sheets, as if a
pressed flower had been squeezed into the linen.

Honora felt inside herself for the blood of the broken hymen.

SIXTEEN

Thus have I had thee, as a dream doth flatter,
In sleep a king, but, waking, no such matter
—Shakespeare

Honora was not seen on dreamside again. It was obvious to the other three that she had made a conscious decision not to return there. It must have taken some struggle. Entry into dreamside had once required considerable discipline and effort; now they were caught in an undertow which delivered them there unasked, and not to be drawn there whenever they slept required serious resistance.

Ella had her suspicions about what was happening. She sensed that Brad Cousins was in some malevolent way responsible, though she was unable to guess why. And he wouldn't be drawn.

"What happened between you two?" she asked for the fifth time. They sat in a pub with ultraviolet strip lighting and a jukebox belting out Motown classics. Brad offered a shrug.

"Don't try to dismiss the question, Brad."

"I'm not *trying* to dismiss the question, I *am* dismissing the question."

"Something happened on dreamside that's made her cut herself off from us, and I know it's something you did."

"How do you know that?"

"Because you've the guts of a sewer rat."

"Ease up Ella," said Lee, bringing in the beer. "Tell us what happened when you went to her room."

"She was in there. I know it. She pretended she wasn't. I even shouted that I knew she was there, but she wouldn't open the door and she wouldn't speak to me." She jabbed a finger dangerously close to Brad's face. "He's responsible."

"It's been nearly five weeks," said Lee.

"You know what it's about, don't you Brad?"

"Get off my back. Go and ask her for Christ's sake."

"No, I'm asking you." Ella turned to Lee. "Honora won't speak to us, so we've only got this reptile to tell us."

Brad suddenly slammed down his pint glass sending a tide of beer cascading across the table. Lee and Ella jumped back. "Why don't you get a muzzle on that rabid mouth of yours, jealous bitch." He stormed out of the bar, slamming a foot into the jukebox and bouncing the stylus into silence.

"You asked for that," said Lee.

Ella had actually paid three unanswered visits to Honora's room. Each time there had been a light on and a radio playing, but Honora had consistently refused to respond. They never saw her around the university campus and she didn't attend lectures.

Visits to dreamside were never quite the same again. There was a marked down-turn in the excitement of just being there. The sense of expectation had died. Before, the place had always been seeded with the scent of honeysuckle. Now it was flat and perfumeless, and troubled by underlying anxieties more felt than understood. They never referred to this anxiety, and the more it went unspoken, the more it grew. Without saying anything, they found themselves resisting the powerful undertow that had been taking them unasked for so long. They were shocked at the effort required to stay away, but eventually their visits thinned out, then dried up completely.

In waking time, things started to go badly for Ella and Lee too. Perhaps this deterioration in their relationship caused the dreamside sag. When it came down to it, the best part of their romance had been conducted on dreamside, and sometimes, now, they were at a loss with each other's ordinariness.

One afternoon Lee looked at Ella, and where he had formerly seen an exotic priestess, there was now some girl with scuffed shoes and hastily applied lipstick.

Ella woke up one morning, and where she had once lain with a young warrior bearing a flaming torch into the dark labyrinths of the psyche, she now found herself in bed alongside a boy with a fluffy beard, who hadn't much to say for himself.

Problems were compounded when Brad "confessed" to Lee that he and Ella had, on occasion, successfully conducted their own dreamtime rendezvous. Lee was genuinely shocked. It had never occurred to him that other dreamtime activities might have been going on in his absence.

"It's a lie," Ella protested, "and it's ridiculous."

"Maybe that's what he meant when he called you jealous."

"I don't believe I'm hearing this! You take in any lie that ape comes out with, and you don't believe a word I say! How can you do that to me?"

Lee let the idea niggle him. Ella was livid. They argued, ridiculously and histrionically, but most of all badly. After that they didn't see each other for over a week.

Lee made the first conciliatory move, driven by some news he had heard in the union bar.

"She did what?" Ella went white.

"She took a load of pills. They had to pump her stomach."

"Oh God! Can we go and see her?"

"Apparently she's already gone home."

"What? Ireland home?"

"Yes, Ireland home."

"When did all this happen?"

"Four or five days ago."

"But what about her course? Her exams?" Lee only shrugged. "Why did I know that something like this was going to happen? We never paid enough attention to her. We were too wrapped up in ourselves."

"Yes."

Ella sat down and began to roll a cigarette. "Please stay with me tonight," she said, without looking up. "I get frightened at night and I'm having bad dreams."

Lee nodded. "You know I want to stay with you."

They made friends again, and made love again. The news about Honora made them vulnerable, and for a while they were gentle with each other.

The day after Lee broke the news, Ella got Honora's home telephone number from the university registrar. Honora's father answered, asked who it was and went to fetch his daughter. He came back on the line to tell her that Honora wasn't well enough to come to the phone, but that she was much better and thank you for calling.

Lee, on going to find out how much Brad knew, discovered that he had cleared out of his bedsit without notice. It had been some time since he had turned in for a lecture, and none of his fellow medical students had seen him in weeks. Lee got Brad's landlady to unlock the door of his room. She stood over him, shaking her keys and listing complaints against student tenants while he inspected the abandoned room. There were a number of medical reference books and a shelf full of sci-fi paperbacks; a battered mono record player and a handful of scratched and sleeveless albums; an oil-fired road-works lantern, a police bollard and the amber dome from a Belisha beacon, plus other trophies and street paraphernalia which for some reason he felt happy to keep in his room; and a few clothes, though all the decent stuff had gone along with his suitcase and bags. There was nothing there he wasn't better off without. Lee told the landlady differently, but he knew for certain that Brad wouldn't be coming back.

With two of them gone, it didn't come as a complete surprise to Lee, when, towards the end of the spring term, a pink handwritten envelope appeared in his room one morning. It had been shoved under the door sometime during the small hours:

Dear Lee,

I still love you but I've got to get my head straightened out. Remember that holiday we planned for the Greek Islands, before everything got heavy? That's where I'm going, I don't know for how long. Maybe I will come back after that and finish my degree, though it's pointless at the moment—I haven't done a stroke of work since I met you and we got mixed up in the dreaming. I haven't got the guts to face you with this, which is why the letter. You're a good man and there will never be any forgetting the things we have done but I've got to get out of it. I'm crying while I'm writing this. I meant that about still loving you. Finish your studies, at least one of us should.

Ella.

Though it was half-expected, Lee was devastated. The four of them had been isolated from the rest of the university, and now he was left completely alone. Honora had been carried out on a stretcher; Brad had bolted; and now Ella had run away to hide. It was exactly a year since he and Ella had come together. He knew he would never get over her.

Like a good boy he stayed at the university and completed his studies. From the end of that term he lived like a monk, got his head down and caught up on a year's neglected reading. He worked hard and was awarded a respectable but undistinguished degree.

He didn't expect to see the others again. Three postcards from Ella arrived in the first couple of months. They showed pictures of brilliantly whitewashed houses against an improbably blue sky, classical temples and definitive Mediterranean sunsets. On their reverse sides were tightly written, difficult-to-read messages with excited descriptions and introspective diversions, all thoroughly impersonal. But Lee kept the postcards and pinned them on his wall close to his pillow as if they would act as a charm against bad dreams and a remedy for spoiled memories. No more arrived.

PART THREE

March 1986

ONE

Crito, we owe a cock to Aesculapius. Please
pay it,
and don't let it pass
—Socrates

"I dreamt it."

"It doesn't seem possible."

"But there it is."

Ella and Honora, heads together, huddle in secrecy in the pan-elled snug of Belfast's Crown, sipping creamy black stout that left thin white moustaches of foam on their upper lips.

"But he was never in your bed, or close to it?"

"Ella, I was dreaming, but I wasn't drunk. I wasn't interested in him. Apart from that dreamthing Brad never got near enough, and neither did anyone else. If it had been *Lee* things could have been different."

"I always knew that you had something for each other."

"I could never have stolen him away from you Ella. He was starry-eyed."

"But this thing with Brad; it was rape."

"Yes. At least that's what I thought then, and for a long time afterwards. But he said I could have stopped it if I'd wanted. It was a mind thing, and I let it happen. I've thought about it a lot since. I don't know if he's right."

"But you were paralyzed; he was stronger and he took advantage. It's no different from the real thing."

"It might as well have been the real thing."

"That's the part that doesn't seem possible."

"You see! Even you doubt me! You've had experience of dreaming, you've been there. You know how it is—but you can't bring yourself to believe that I got pregnant because of something that happened on dreamside. Maybe she was drunk, maybe she can't remember, maybe she just doesn't want to admit it, I've had plenty of time to try them all on. How could I expect anyone else to accept this, if you of all people can't see it?"

"Honora, I do believe you; I have to believe you. Like you said, I've got some experience of this, but even for me it seems like a long time ago and sometimes I don't even know how much of it was true."

"It was all true, all right. The pregnancy was confirmed, absolutely. No question of error."

"But you lost the baby? It miscarried? Was that before or after you took an overdose?"

"After. It was the pregnancy that made me do it. I was going mad. You don't know what it was like. I thought I might have the baby; then I thought it might be born with two heads or not even human at all. And me a good Catholic girl. At least, I was then. Anyway, the suicide attempt induced the miscarriage. It was finished."

Ella put a hand on Honora's.

"You'd best be moving if you really want to catch that ferry. Will you let me know what Lee found out about you-know-who? Though I'll tell you something Ella, I didn't have a bad dream or a *repeater* while you were here. Maybe they've stopped again after all. God help us, I hope so."

"I hope so too Honora. Now, no more grieving about lost babies, OK? Promise?"

"No more grieving. I mean, if she were out there now, she'd for-give me, wouldn't she?"

"Just try not to think about it."

"Right. No more grieving."

"You'll come over to England and see us?"

"I'll try."

"I don't want try, I want promise."

"Perhaps when I get a few days' holiday . . . Easter."

"Easter. That's a promise and I'll keep you to it."

Outside the Crown they walked to the car park and kissed, something they would never have done in student days. Age softens as much as it hardens, thought Ella. She got into her Midget and raced back.

She arrived at Lee's cottage before midnight. He had heard the car and was standing silhouetted in the doorway. The hall was spiced with the smell of the curry which simmered on the stove, a hint of whiskey on Lee as Ella squeezed his hand and went by him into the lounge.

He poured strong drinks and served up the curry. They caught up in shorthand, then finished the meal in silence. Ella took her glass and sat on the floor in front of the open fire while Lee massaged her aching shoulders. The fire sparked and flickered hypnotically.

"So it could be him?" Ella said lazily.

"It could be; he's fallen into a well. I never got near enough to second-guess him. It wasn't the fond reunion. He's been that way so long his face has gone whiskey colored."

"But he's had *the dreams?*"

"Oh, he's had *the dreams* all right; there was a very scared Brad inside that alcohol. He made a little speech about unwanted visitors, but I didn't know whether he was talking about me or the dreams."

"But is he bringing them on? Has he been back there?"

"That's the question. Whatever it is, he seems to think that they've started to get up and walk. He kept staring out of his window at the empty cottage next door. Looking for enemies."

"What did your instincts say?"

"Too frightened. What about her?"

"She was definitely holding out on me. I'm sure it's her. She gave me as much of the story as she thought would keep me satisfied. Rationed it out, right up until the end. But there's more, I'm sure of it."

"So it's Honora."

"I could be wrong."

"It's all we've got to go on. So how was the journey?"

"I had some bad feelings on the way over. Then when I got to Ireland it was OK. Honora was warm after she'd recovered from the shock of seeing me. It brought a lot of things back."

"Me too. Seeing Brad, even in that state."

"It brought back things about us, too."

"All of it?"

"Everything."

Lee kissed Ella's neck. "I never really figured why or how it ended."

"Well," Ella smiled, "we never really forgave each other for being only human."

"One day you were gone, then there were three postcards, and then thirteen years had passed."

"The postcards! I remember trying to fill them with anything but what really mattered."

They lapsed into silence. Ella suddenly felt Lee's loneliness dangerously close to the surface.

"You were never out of my mind. All the years."

"Stop talking about it. Come here. We can make the years fall away." She smiled again, and put her hand inside his shirt. "Do you remember a certain game we used to play?"

"Of course I remember."

Ella pulled him down on to the rug and they made love. It was clean, hungry sex. They pretended nothing had changed, that they were back in Ella's scented cave and that the amber light from the fire was the dawn breaking through the heavy curtains of their old world. They could be childlike again. They could pretend to be victims of a fold in the ordinary sequence of time, with the intervening thirteen years as a long cold night. Pretending was good, and each could pretend as well as the other, and the game of pretending didn't devour the way that dreaming devoured.

T W O

"Ditto, ditto!" cried Tweedledee
—Lewis Carroll

Honora Brennan, still recovering from Ella's unexpected visit, is frightened. She wanders round the house drinking from a glass of stout and swallowing temazepam. In her back room she stands before the covered easel and removes the tablecloth.

Sitting back on a high stool, she contemplates her work, squinting at it through the soft-focus lens of stout and temazepam which gives the painting a fluid quality all of its own. The canvas shows a familiar scene: a sturdy, spreading oak leaning out across a lake that seems to have no farther shore. But the view is changed in some way, as if Honora has painted a different dreamside, one in the grip of a new authority, which leaves even her guessing.

Honora covers up the painting before the answer comes to her. She climbs the stairs to bed. The hinge on the gate outside whines and she glances down into the street. A child has climbed on to her gate and is swinging on it, gently back and forth: a girl, a little older than those she teaches at school, neglected, wearing a cut-down dress from a fashion at least a decade past, with lank hair framing sad eyes. The girl looks up at her. Honora draws the curtains.

Curled up in the dark, Honora wishes that Ella had stayed longer. Maybe she *would* go to England, and spend some time with

Ella. Her visit has turned up buried secrets, memories that sit up and point at her like corpses out of coffins; but it has also brought the warm companionship they enjoyed in the early days on dreamside.

Honora spends half the night drifting between waking, sleeping and dreaming. She is shaken by the wind rattling the window. Ella, Lee, Brad, Professor Burns and countless other voices all take turns at owning the hand that rattles the window, until in exasperation she gets out of bed. Taking a school copy of the prayer book from her bookshelf she levers open the staples that bind it, carefully folding the leaves into paper wedges and forcing them between the gaps of the window frame. She climbs into bed and drifts back into sleep.

The familiar branches of the giant oak loom large, as if from out of a mist, swaying gently and beckoning her on; she's carried in by the currents. She just goes with it, not part of it but with it, that's all it ever took, all it ever wanted, without struggle or without any more need to help it along, until, breaking into substance like the gentle breaking of an insignificant wave upon a beach it is delivered to you, or you to it.

But this is not the same dreamside. The oak is dead, the willow a cluster of bony twigs in ugly gestures; the trampled grass a crust of hard frost; and the lake itself a solid, frozen feet-thick sheet of ice.

This is the dreamside that Honora has been visiting these last twelve months, searching for something she doesn't understand. She patrols the lakeside looking out across the frozen water for signs that never come. She walks clear out onto the frozen lake about twenty, thirty yards. Her boot scrapes the sprinkled layer of snow: the ice underneath is a grey paste with impenetrable darkness immediately beneath it.

Then, as before, she hears the dull thump of an explosion under the ice: *dooomphh* way out from the shore; a thud, maybe, of ice shifting and resettling. There it goes again, *doooomphh*, only nearer this time. Honora is spooked by the sound, even though she's heard it before a thousand times.

For the first time (though every time she comes it's for the first time) Honora sees hairline cracks in the ice, though it's feet thick with no sign of a thaw. She sees more shadowy movements beneath the ice, strange shapes forming and reforming, something live. DOOOOOMMPH! There goes that noise again, much closer this time, and she feels the ice shiver beneath her. What thing is under the ice, thrashing around, trying to get out?

Honora bends down to take a closer look then—DOOOOOMMPH!!—that thudding explosion happens right under her feet and this time she feels the ice shaking beneath her and is almost thrown off balance. She sees a large crack opening up and zigzagging towards her, passing between her legs, racing towards the shore. Now the crack is opening up wide and Honora begins to run, slipping as she goes, her legs becoming paralyzed as she tries to escape the opening ice behind her. Her running slows. Her muscles freeze. The ice is locking in to her. She is becoming ice herself. Only by a monumental effort of will is she able to throw herself on to the shore, and out of the dream.

She wakes up in a temazepam-and-stout-induced sweat, wishing for someone to hold, to speak to, the someone she denies herself by way of self-punishment. She even contemplates phoning Ella and making a clean breast of it. She picks up the clock. It's 4:40 A.M. Maybe she will go over to England, to see if Ella and Lee can help her with this madness. She sinks back down on to the pillow, hoping for unviolated sleep, clean in the knowledge that the dream, like the little girl swinging on the gate, won't call on her in the same night twice.

THREE

In the dreamer's dream, the dreamed one awoke
—Jorge Luis Borges

Nothing has been said exactly, but Ella stays at Lee's. Both think leave it, wait and see, bad luck to use words on it. They sleep together, curled up like two question marks, one sleeping body cupping the other, resisting the dream.

Lee goes back to his office where he tries to work, struggling against exhaustion and fear. Ella waits at home, reading paperbacks and doing uncharacteristically wifely things: cleaning, shopping, cooking dinner and giving him a neck rub when he gets back from work. In return, Lee fixes the hood of the car.

Then, one night, their resistance collapses and they find each other on dreamside. The dream is lucid and with the same feverish excitement as at any time before, but they wrap their arms about each other's waists as if the other might dissolve at any moment. They stare around in horror at their idyll: the charred branches, the barren soil, the icy lake . . .

There is nothing to say in the face of this sterility, and immediately the dream breaks.

"What happened?" they ask, waking. They have always regarded dreamside as a private island and a personal haven, despite the menace that shadowed their later dreaming. It has always been held to be a place beyond change.

"But what happened?"

That morning, Ella got a call from Honora. She had decided to spend Easter with them. She had booked a flight from Belfast to Birmingham. Ella was to drive to the airport and collect her.

Honora was shy with Lee when they returned. "Twelve years? Can it really be twelve years?"

"Nearly thirteen. You look great," said Lee. She didn't. Honora looked pale and her blue veins stood out too prominently on her forehead and hands. Her eyes lacked sheen.

Of course it's her, he thought, just look at her.

They talked the evening away, without mentioning the dreaming. The subject itched to be scratched, but Ella was patient. She knew that Honora had come to tell her something, and she waited for the moment to be right.

That moment came the next day. Ella had arranged to take Honora for a drive, anything to distract from the burden of anticipation. In the morning they drove to Warwick Castle, and crept giggling around the dungeons and waxworks. In the afternoon they visited Coventry cathedral, where the giant new building stands shoulder to shoulder with the war-blitzed shell of the medieval Gothic version. Inside the ruin, Honora turned to face the altar with its cross of charred beams.

"I had it," she said. "You knew, didn't you?"

"The baby miscarried. You lost the baby."

Honora turned to face her. "I lost the baby. I also had the baby."

"What *are* you talking about, Honora?"

"I had the baby and I didn't have the baby. You still don't understand? Do you need me to spell it out for you?"

"Maybe I do. Maybe I'm not as clever as you think."

They stood facing each other, Ella searching Honora's disappointed eyes until suddenly, she understood.

"On *dreamside?*"

Honora didn't flicker.

"You had it on *dreamside?* It couldn't be!" Ella suddenly felt out of her depth. She was first to look away.

"Are you sure it wasn't . . ."

"Wasn't what? A dream?"

Ella took the other woman's arm. "Let's go. I need to sit down somewhere and think about this."

They walked across the hollowed-out shell of the old cathedral, down the steps and out across the face of the defiant new monument. They found a bench. Honora stared downwards.

Have it? How can you have it and not have it? But that's how it was.

"It was November. Cold November. Ma and Da thought I was going mad. Maybe I was . . . I remember everything. Mostly I remember how cold it was. Bitter winds and mists rolling down from the loughs. Rain. All that.

"It was my barren year. My lost year. After I'd tried to kill myself at university, I was just idle. I felt . . . cauterized. All nerves gone. Spring and summer slipped into autumn and I didn't even notice. Ma and Da fussing over me the whole time, I had to shut them out to stay sane. There was a weekly appointment with a psychologist. A nice man. I told him everything about myself. I opened up to him like a flower, told him all about my childhood, all that stuff. And in all the candor he didn't see I'd kept this other thing quiet."

"You didn't tell him about dreamside?"

"Not a thing."

"Didn't he guess you were hiding something?"

"I don't know. I kept him busy with masses and masses of information about other things. It just came pouring out. It seemed to keep him satisfied. But the more I talked, the more I kept it a secret, the more I could feel it swelling inside me. I knew I had an appointment on dreamside. It was inflating me, insisting, summoning me.

"I stopped fighting it, and then one night I was back there. You know, it's funny: it was always night, and I couldn't change it. And the moon was always full, and on dreamside I had this huge, soft, roundness growing inside me. It was all different. A cold place. Frost, and moonwashed nights, and trees all silhouette. And the lake was calm, like oil.

"I was terrified, Ella. Every time I was drawn back there, I was bigger. I tried to hold it off. Have you ever tried to stay awake, days at a time? Try it. You start to break up. First there are little slips, with your words faltering and fusing together. Then there's all the dithering, unable to perform simple tasks. And you lose concentration, you're 'away' somewhere else; and then you start to laugh at yourself, but with hysterical laughter that cuts back at you. You forget why you're trying to stay awake. So that's what you do, fight it, fight it. In the end, of course, you give in.

"Then I arrived there with the awful realization, you know, this is the time, this is the moment. It was so cold there. And there was something else . . . a shadow . . . a bad echo. The trees were ugly charcoal silhouettes and the moon was like a gob of candle wax dribbled across the lake. I was thinking I would rather be anywhere but here when I felt the first contraction. It was like a shock wave. Instinct took over, and I looked for somewhere to crouch. I went over to the oak. I couldn't get this idea out of my head that I was like an animal, looking at the moon; like a she-wolf about to whelp.

"I thought about my body, sleeping in my bedroom. But what was the point? I couldn't stop it. Hours seemed to pass. There was no light, no dawn. Only pain. Loneliness and pain. Then the waters broke. I grabbed hold of my knees and held my breath. The contractions came every two minutes.

"I leaned back on my hands and I could feel the baby's head, pushing, pushing. I was delirious, I thought the dream would have to break: no, it's impossible, it won't come, there's really nothing to come, but then there it was. Red-hot iron searing at my insides. I was shivering with fear or pain or cold. I couldn't stop shivering. Then my bowels moved and I couldn't control it. I stopped pushing and I had to open my mouth to get some air in. Then when I pushed again, the baby's head shot out. I was biting the air for breath.

"The rest of the baby came in a slippery, blubbery heap. I knew I was weeping and gulping and shivering, but I did everything on instinct. I cleared out its mouth with my finger and then it gulped at the air and began to cry. I was actually holding the baby in my hands. After a while there were more contractions as the afterbirth came away. I held my breath and pushed it out. Then I laid the baby on the ground, bit the cord and knotted it as if I'd done it a hundred times. I took the baby and walked into the lake, up to my knees. It was very cold. I washed the baby clean, and then I washed myself.

"The baby was whole, pure, clean; and beautiful. So beautiful that I remember sobbing over her, from exhaustion and relief. Then the dream broke."

Ella let out a deep breath. "You went through it alone. All alone."

"There's no midwifery there, Ella."

"But we went back there. We could never find you. Or you never came."

"I never came to you. But I couldn't stop it. On dreamside I grew bigger, even though there was nothing physical showing here. I carried it. I carried it and I delivered it."

"But you never told me anything. We could have helped. We could have done something."

"But I didn't want you, Ella. Not any of you, and least of all him. God, I can't even speak his name. I delivered the child in that place, under that tree, and I did it with a scream and a curse that had the place shivering. God help me, when that child came out I named it a curse on him, a blasted curse in all the mess and pain and blood. I know it was a terrible thing to do, and I know that curses come back on you, but that's what I felt. I cursed it in his name and I cursed him in its name.

"Remember that time on dreamside when you swore at Brad— and didn't he deserve it!—but it came out like a real thing? Words like real things? Well, I did the same and I offered the tiny soul of that dreamside baby to the curse I put on Brad Cousins."

"But in the end it's only words, Honora. Words are not real things. They're only words."

"Not on dreamside they're not. Words *are* things there. I cursed the baby and I washed it, and then I wished the baby away. Then the dream broke."

"As they always did."

"Yes."

"And did you ever go back?"

"Never voluntarily. I was dragged back. I don't know if something was pulling me or whether I was unconsciously driving myself back there to look for it. Anyway, it was never there."

Ella gazed thoughtfully at the cathedral spire pricking at the blue sky. "Do you still go to mass?" she asked suddenly.

"What? You're joking. I haven't been since."

"Since it all happened?"

"Yes."

"You used to be a strong Catholic; do you think this could be why you keep returning to dreamside?"

"I never said I did."

"No, you never said you did. Honora, you should go to mass."

Honora shook her head, puzzled.

"I see it. Tomorrow's Good Friday. You must go to Catholic Mass."

"Don't you go making plans for me. I haven't been near a church since my university days and I'll not go to one tomorrow nor any other day."

"It's important. I know it!"

"Listen to you! An atheist, telling me to get to church!"

"I'm not claiming to be a believer; for you it's different."

"I lost my faith years ago, and I feel better off without it, thanks all the same."

"I don't believe it; you know what they say, 'once a Catholic' . . ."

"What do *you* know about being a Catholic?"

"I know that you've had an experience that might be enough to derange someone else, and that you're still carrying around terrible feelings about that baby you lost—"

"*Aborted.*"

"That's your word, not mine. And it's exactly the point: you can't come to terms with that guilt, so back you go to dreamside, night after night, trying to deal with it, wanting to block it out so much you think or dream or know you've delivered on dreamside. I'm talking about *guilt* Honora, something your church knows all about, and it offers you a way out. I'm the first person you've told in thirteen years. You've got to find someone you can confess it to, someone who means more to you than me. You've got to go to confession!"

"That's all very pat; but you've no understanding of the things you're speaking about. For one, I've no faith and no belief, it doesn't mean anything to me any more—"

"Maybe not consciously; but isn't that the point?"

"And secondly, you've no conception of what it means to walk into confession and cheerfully announce, besides a few venial slips, an avalanche of mortal sin. Oh no Father I haven't been to mass in thirteen years, no not even on Good Fridays, and then there's this small matter of the abortion or induced miscarriage call it what you will, and besides that the wee question of attempted suicide. Everyone a roaster, guaranteed apoplexy for the priest. Forget it."

"It's your only way out."

"Ella, I said forget it."

They drove back to Lee's house in gloomy silence. Lee was dumb enough to ask what was wrong.

"Talk to her," Ella said as soon as Honora's back was turned, "she's more open to you."

But Ella finally relayed the whole story, while Honora sulked in her room. Lee sat in silence and despaired. He was beginning to have serious doubts about everything. He understood that Honora was neurotic and began to have second thoughts about Ella's state of mind. He was afraid of the drama these two mad women were creating, and wanted to stay well clear. Ella was still applying her usual methods to force him into carrying out her will. He was looking for a suitable opportunity to put his foot down, and thought that this was it.

"I'm not sure what you're asking me to do," he said, "but if she's saying no to the idea, then it just won't work."

"It's guilt; honest, natural, inevitable, abscess-forming guilt. It just needs draining. Lance it with confession, out comes the pus, stitch it up. That's what the Catholic Church is for, and that's what she's missing. End of dreams. Talk to her; she'll listen to you."

"If she says she doesn't believe any more, then you have to accept it. You can't resurrect people's faith for them. It's not like renewing your membership down at the tennis club."

"She's a Catholic; she's not Sunday School C of E like us. It's scorched into them from an early age."

"I won't ask her to do it."

"What's the matter with you? It makes no difference if she feels she's lost her faith. She's Catholic through and through. She's like a stick of seaside rock with the letters running through."

"Or the wick running through the candle, is what the priests told us," said Honora, appearing behind them. "I've thought some more. Maybe you're right. At least I'll try."

Ella smiled, but only at Lee.

F O U R

*When I say, My bed shall comfort me, my couch
shall ease my complaint; then thou scarest me with
dreams, and terrifiest me through visions*
—Job

It was Good Friday. Honora had protested seven changes of
heart, but Ella had managed to deliver her that afternoon to a small
modern Catholic church near by. Ella watched her go in with her
head bowed, and sat waiting in the car with the radio turned up.

Inside, Honora sat through the service with a hardened resistance. She dutifully kissed the cross when called, and took the sacra-
ment, though mechanically, feeling nothing. But in the confessional
she asked for the young priest's blessing and revealed the entire
story in terms of a catalogue of sin until the priest, at last realizing
the depth of her distress, asked her to stop.

She emerged from the church and got into Ella's car.

"Well?"

"It's a bit like going to the dentist after a long absence. I've got to
go back tomorrow and have some more done."

"Is that usual?"

"Only for us very bad mortal sinners," she smiled. "Actually, it
was me; I asked if he would talk to me tomorrow. There was a
whole row of people ready with their fictitious confessions, and I
was holding them up."

"What's he like?"

"Young. Quite nice."

"Tasty?"

"Get on, Ella. He's a priest!"

Ella was relieved that Honora could be light. They had a private joke about the priest, which they kept from Lee, who wanted to know what they were giggling about. That night Honora slept deep and free of the pull of dreamside. It was the first time since the dreaming had started up again.

In the morning, Ella drove to the church, watched Honora go in, and waited in the car again.

But Lee had not been free of dreams. Although spared the direct dreamside experience, he'd spent feverish nights in the grip of anxiety. Now there were two strange women in his house, conspiring to draw him into complex plans of action, all based around phantom events. Something was closing on him, something he'd held off for a long time. Ella and Honora, just by being there in his house, opened the crack between the worlds and made him believe in things he'd had to work hard to dismiss. They undermined his sealed, ordered world.

Still Lee maintained incredulity at Honora's story of dreamside conception and delivery, but Ella had refused to let him challenge the idea.

"Get a grip on reality," he had urged.

"You've forgotten everything you learned," Ella hissed. "Try telling that to Honora. In reality, in the dream, in the mind," prodding her own head for effect with an angry, stiff finger, "you're sure you know the difference?"

"There's a clear difference. A very clear difference."

"Is there?"

Lee had remained awake for some hours, staring into the gloomy shadows of the darkened bedroom, looking for very clear differences.

But it was only when he had the house to himself that he had the space to think things through. He wanted to chart his own course. After all, who was this Ella? Not the same person he knew thirteen years ago, in the days when the desire to believe anything (so long as it was bizarre enough) far outweighed any interest in seeing things clearly. Lee had heard precious little about what had happened in the intervening period, only that it was X-rated. What was he supposed to make of that? And what was he to think about being rewritten into the script? So much had happened to them; they couldn't possibly be the people they once were.

But why had it taken only moments to put the clock back, make love on the rug and reopen this obsession with dreaming? The answer to that, he knew, was Ella: it was what Ella wanted. He only ever seemed to figure passively. She blew into his house like a high wind, undressed on his rug and stood over him: she slept in his bed and she made him dream again. Then after that she dragged poor ill Honora all the way over from Ireland to be mad in the house with them.

Lee began to suspect that it might be Ella, after all, who was in the business of dream resurrection. He strode out to the garden shed and emerged with a stepladder. He brought it indoors and set it up on the landing directly beneath the hatch to the attic. Then he went off in search of a torch.

Inside the church Father Boyle was watering a vase of irises. Otherwise the church was empty. On a blue wall, painted in golden lettering were the words HERE I AM LORD.

He was a couple of years younger than her, with a freckle face and close-cropped sandy hair. His piercing blue eyes were moist with enthusiasm. Honora had only ever experienced priestly powers vested in men much older. She had never been expected to respect the spiritual authority of someone younger than herself.

He looked up as he heard the door close. "Come in, Honora; see, I didn't forget you. You know, a funny thing happened last night. I went to sleep and I had a dream, well it was all mixed up; but the thing is, I knew that I was dreaming." He set down his watering can with a bump.

"At least, that was the only thing that was clear. What do you make of that? Isn't that something like you were saying to me yesterday?"

"Something like that, Father." It seemed slightly ridiculous to call this smiling boy "father."

"Do you want to tell me again? Not as in the confession; I think we dealt with that—as far as I understood it to be a mountain of mortal sins." He seemed to make light of it. "But I got a bit confused about whether or not these sins were actually committed or dreamed about."

"You're not going to be much clearer whichever way I tell it."

"Try me."

She could see that he wanted to help. Not in the ritualized way of the priests she remembered, or at least not just in that manner, but through some more earthly, human contract. He looked even younger than she had at first thought as he leaned towards her solicitously. Suddenly he said, "Put aside what may be sin or sinning—you're here and I'm here, let's talk it through."

"You're kind, Father. Here goes." Honora took the priest through the story, leaving out nothing. He listened attentively, nodding throughout and stroking his beardless chin. He interrupted her only twice; once to clarify what she had said about the discovery of hymenal blood, and then to ask her for some details concerning her attempted suicide.

"You probably think I need a psychiatrist, not a priest," said Honora.

"Not at all."

"Yes you do. You think I'm an hysteric."

"No. I'll admit I'm baffled, bewildered, confused by what you've told me. It goes beyond my . . . beyond the range of my confessional. But I have to believe in your unburdening."

They were silent for a while. The priest coughed and started uncertainly, "A lot of people, when they want to . . . unburden, can't face the realization of their own sin. They often tell me that they weren't . . . in possession of themselves at the time. They were drunk, perhaps had taken drugs, or sometimes they tell me they were sleepwalking or in a trance, a daze, a fog; and occasionally they tell me . . ."

"They thought they were dreaming." Honora looked away.

"I'm sorry. I didn't mean to be so banal."

"It's not in my head, Father. There are other people who were involved who can tell you; I've already said that. One of them is sitting outside in a car waiting for me."

"The other woman—is she a Catholic?"

"Ha!"

"But it was her idea for you to come? Interesting!"

"The point is that if it was just me, I might believe that I was off my head; but there were a number of others involved. We weren't hallucinating, or drunk, or stoned, and in those days we were all reasonably sane God forgive us, we were just . . . dreaming, *dreaming,* I want to say dreaming but there should be another word for what was happening!"

"I was just trying to fit things into a way of understanding it."

"Don't try! I've been trying for thirteen years and all it gives you is the shakes before you go to bed at night."

"Do you believe in the sins of omission as in those of commission?" said the priest.

"Of course," said Honora, "that is I understand the difference. As for belief, well I don't know where I am with that these days."

"The sins of commission, the things we have done wrong, belong to the world as it is, as we have made it. The sins of omission, the things we have failed to do, belong to the world as it might have been. Isn't it the same with your dreams? They belong not to this world as it is, but as it might have been."

"But the miscarriage . . . and I tried to kill myself. That was all real."

"Honora, perhaps everything is a dream," he leaned his face closer to hers, still smiling, "but a dream in the mind of God.

"Consider," he said. Heavy spots of rain began to fall, tapping loudly on the roof. Honora made an effort to concentrate. "Consider that the world, the universe, is a dream in the mind of God. When He awakes, it's all over. But maybe it's not a universe, but a multiverse, what about that? You know, dreams within dreams within dreams, smaller and smaller or larger and larger whichever way you like. Meanwhile, us sinners go about our business in His dream, dreaming ourselves. Here's where it gets complicated. If our dreams are out of our control, that's one thing: and wasn't it Saint Augustine who thanked God that he was not responsible for his own dreams! But if we start to be able to control our dreams, and therefore are able to choose between sinful and righteous acts at this other level, that's another. Only in the multiverse, you would have to make a choice. Which level, I mean. And you would choose Him and His dream."

"Are you telling me it doesn't matter what happens in the dream world, even if you know what you are doing? That there's no right or wrong in the kind of dream world that I'm telling you about?"

"I'm telling you that God has placed it beyond the range of our theology," he said, still smiling.

"Father, has the Church changed at all in the last thirteen years?"

"Why do you ask that?"

"Because you don't sound like the priests I used to know in Ireland. I mean, are you sure, about this dreaming thing, that there's nothing . . . *demonic?*"

"Is that what they taught you in Ireland?"

"No. I didn't mean that."

"Then I wish you hadn't said it." His lovely boyish smile had faded. He went cold on her. "Look, I thought we could better exorcize . . . pardon me, chase away these dreams of yours by talking it through. If you prefer we could pray and I could give you a penance."

The priest made this last remark as if he were a village GP offering to prescribe colored water to another doctor. Honora felt as though she had let him down. "Whatever you think best, Father," she said meekly.

"Let's kneel together under the statue of Our Lady," he said gently, evidently reconciled to the idea. They went and kneeled together in the shadows of an alcove, under a plastic statue of the Virgin Mary. It frightened Honora a little. It was too realistic, the blue-robed, white-cowled icon hovering over her, one hand raised in doubtful benediction. It seemed to glow slightly in the candlelight of the darkened alcove. She avoided its gaze.

"Close your eyes," said the priest, "and I want you to think of these dreams. Then I want you to empty your mind of them, and fill it with thoughts of God."

With Ella and Honora out of the house Lee found it easier to discount anything he had ever believed about dreams. When you added it up it didn't amount to so much. These recent disclosures about a dreamside *conception* and a dreamside *birthright* . . . it was all so far back. At best he wouldn't be prepared to swear that they didn't invent most of it, or, to be more accurate, didn't deceive themselves into believing things. The point was that they had all wanted to believe in it, badly wanted it. So when you came to check it out, what exactly happened?

There was the undeniable fact that some kind of out-of-body liaisons were taking place, and at some consciously agreed location which they had come to call dreamside; but the corroboration of this could only ever happen after the event. Maybe the agreements they all reached were not concerned with a secondary plane on which real experiences took place, but were no more than the result of a rough telepathy in the group. Certainly the results achieved in the days when the professor was around would square with this theory. It was only after the death of Professor Burns, when discipline was lost and things started to slip, that the whole experience went haywire.

As for the four of them, hell they were so wrapped up in their bloody experiments that they hardly spoke to another soul. They were always prepared to support—uncritically—the most outrageous claims about what could be accomplished. A classic case of isolation sustaining a group delusory system. Was there a real basis for thinking that anything had happened at all? Had they just fired themselves up into a frenzy of delusion?

He climbed the stepladder and pushed open the trap door to the attic. He switched on the torch and flashed the beam around the unplastered walls. There was something there he wanted, something he'd stored there years before, after dreaming had been forgotten—or had been pretended to be forgotten . . . Lee's attic had not been disturbed for years. Opening the hatch was like breaking into someone's sleep.

In the most recent episode of dreaming, when he and Ella had accidentally drifted back to dreamside, they had not found the place where all their previous rendezvous had occurred but somewhere different. This confirmed for him that dreamside was not a real place, but a projection. Sometimes our needs are so strong, he thought, they will stop the sky from falling.

And now Honora claimed to have left something behind on dreamside. Plainly she was ill.

Making love on dreamside: what was that all about? He and Ella had been so obsessed with the projection of their relationship on this other level that their real relationship, the one made of blood and tears, had been eclipsed. Perhaps it had all been a way of making themselves seem more important. Incense and candlelight can only ever transform the cave so far. Then you need help in the fantasy game, and they had gone out and called in the heavy artillery.

Lee crossed the attic floor carefully, stepping from one unboarded joist to another. At the far side was a tea chest draped by an old blanket. A small dust storm billowed up in the beam of the torch as he removed the cover.

Brad snorting, sweating, turned in a fever somewhere between sleep and stupor, swimming against a tide that pulls him back and back to that dreaded place. His sea of sleep is full of sharks these days and he gulps down mouthfuls of salt water as he swims frenziedly. He woke up shivering and felt a warm patch turning icy on his leg. He'd pissed himself again in his sleep.

Through the window all he could see was the mist rolling in from the moors. It was 11 A.M., Easter Saturday, and the mist had laid thick trails of moisture over the grass outside and had breathed vaporous patterns on the windows. He was cold. He looked for the tiny cone of blue flame in his single paraffin heater and saw that it had gone out. He buried his head in his hands and allowed himself the luxury of tears.

Then he remembered Lee Peterson. Or was that all another dream? Another bad dream? He had woken up on the sofa to find Lee standing over him like a boxer who'd just put him on the canvas. Thirteen years older and looking more, gone a bit porky, with hair thinning and face fattening, stiff with respectability, but more than that, looking like someone who had never been capable of dreaming in his life.

"Wherever you came from, fuck off back there." He said it to the snakes and scorpions of his delusions and it always seemed to do the trick.

But Peterson had been there in the flesh: he'd left a business card on the mantelpiece. Brad read it and tossed it away in disgust. He couldn't remember the details of their conversation, but he did know what it was about. No doubt Lee had some kind of an angle on the things that were stirring on dreamside; and that bitch Ella Innes was probably mixed up in it somewhere too. Brad leaned against the windowsill and blinked at the squat, derelict cottage across the yard.

It was shrouded in mist, but someone was looking back at him through one of the broken windows. He had to squint to make it out in the poor visibility, but it was a face he knew. He thought he might race across the yard and grab her by the hair; but he knew that by then she would be gone. She was always gone. The face at the window vanished.

"Why won't you *talk* with me?"

The mist rolled over the yard, muffling all sound. Brad saw a tiny light flicker and then go out in the upper windows of the cottage.

"Dreamwalkers."

Sometimes he saw blue and yellow sparks through the windows, and red glowing embers in midair. He'd had dreams about the cottage: elementals came up through the earth and into the house, crossing over the threshold of dreams and into the realm of waking life, childlike, malignant, massing for an attack, bursting and spilling across the world. Every time he allowed himself to sleep he feared he gave the dreamwalkers more power, more time to marshal their forces, a route across an unguarded bridge from one realm to another. He saw the light flicker again. He pushed his feet into some shoes, grabbed an almost empty bottle of whiskey and rushed out into the yard.

"Wherever you come from, fuck off back there!" he bellowed, draining his bottle and flinging it at the cottage. It smashed and the light went out. "I know your game. It was me that let you in; it's me can send you back! *Back!*"

Lurching back inside, he grabbed the can of paraffin and marched across the yard to the cottage. Hanging from broken hinges, the door was wedged open. He squeezed inside. Bricks, rubble and fallen plaster obstructed his progress, and he stumbled and climbed over the debris in darkness, stirring the smell of decomposing plaster. There was a wild scuffling in the shadows.

"Rats, bats and dreamwalkers," he muttered.

Groping his way, he found the staircase and set foot on the first step. The house reeked of dry rot. He was afraid his weight might send him crashing down to the cellar. At the top a door stood ajar. He pushed and saw broken rafters, and black puddles on the floorboards; gaping holes to the floor below. He turned to the other door.

In the second room, windows, ceiling and floorboards were all intact and unbroken. It was tidy, swept, and on its walls someone had hung a poster and a few bleached, twisted shapes of wood as ornament. Opposite the door, huddled in a single sleeping bag and clinging to each other in terror were two young people, boy and girl, sitting with their backs to the wall, their wide eyes like huge silver coins in the grey light.

"Human form," said Brad from the doorway.

"We're not hurting anything," said the girl.

"Dreamwalkers! What's your name? Quick now!"

"Victoria."

"Victoria," mimicking her squeaky voice. "No it's not, it's Honora Brennan. What's your name lad?"

"Keith."

"No it's not, your name is Brad Cousins. Dreamwalkers!"

"He's drunk," said the girl.

"Issat your little girl? Eh? Eh? Is she yours?"

"What girl?"

"Don't play with me, son. Is she yours? Dreamwalkers? Little girl eaters?"

He marched into the room, twisting the top off the paraffin can.

"Whoever you think we are, we're not!" shouted the youth.

Brad stopped for a moment and looked at him. Then he shook his head. "I can't take the risk." He started flinging the paraffin around the room.

"Jesus, is that petrol? Vicky get up!" The two students grabbed their clothes and the sleeping bag and fled naked out of the room. Brad emptied the can before discarding it, struck a match and dropped it on the spilled paraffin. Then he followed them down the stairs and out into the yard, where they were struggling into their jeans. His breath reared in the mist.

"Stay and watch," Brad invited generously. "Burn her up!"

But they declined, running down the road as they buttoned their clothes. Brad waved goodbye and turned, with enormous satisfaction, to watch the growing blaze.

While Honora was inside the church wrestling with the young priest's theology, Ella yawned and stretched and fiddled with the car radio. Something crackled and stuttered through the wavebands, a child-woman's voice, singing:

> And your dreams are like dollar bills
> in the pocket of a gambler
> and they whisper in your ear
> like those good-time girls

Ella tried to catch a better reception, but the signal drifted out again. She snapped off the radio and was startled to see someone looking at her through the passenger window. It was a girl, standing in the rain a few yards away from the car. Their eyes met. She was pale and thin, not quite into her teens and wearing what looked like left-overs from a church jumble sale. She had a bruised look, the eyes of a kid who has taken a beating for stealing sweets. Ella, soft on street waifs everywhere, instantly felt a surge of pity. Wanting to give the girl something, she reached for her purse and got out of the car.

But the girl had gone. Ella looked up and down the street: nothing. She looked at the closed doors of the church and shrugged before climbing back into her car, shielding herself from the increasingly heavy rain.

She settled back behind the steering wheel before realizing that something had been written in the condensation on the inside of the windscreen. Water droplets had collected and dripped from the crudely formed letters to the foot of the glass. The words said HELP ME.

Prompted by a movement, Ella glanced from the words to her rear-view mirror. Then she turned to look across her shoulder. Now the girl stood by the doors of the church. She opened the door and looked back at Ella, as if inviting her to follow. When she entered the church, Ella got out of the car and went in after her.

Lee, in the attic, lifted from the chest bundles of note books, ring-binders full of papers, photograph albums, a couple of half-completed diaries. Then the smaller stuff like posters and tickets for college dances, academic year photographs and other university flotsam, old poems that now made his skin crawl, theater programs, a signed publicity shot of an unfamous female rock singer to *Lee love from Carla Black, great fun XXX*, letters from old friends. From the bottom of the tea chest he lifted a perspex case.

He hardly dared open it. Could things be said to have happened only so long as they agreed they had happened? Perhaps all that had gone on between Ella and him was the grand performance—what had the professor called it? *folie à deux*—a teenage romance conducted against a blazing operatic backdrop of erected just to give things stature. Maybe that was it: nothing more than an outlandish metaphor for adolescent love.

He balanced the torch on the corner of the chest and broke open the perspex case. It contained a girl's black beret; a half-empty packet of Rizla liquorice cigarette papers, a brass incense-trinket, half a dozen color-faded photographs of Ella or of himself with Ella, and three postcards from the Greek Islands. It was his shrine to Ella. Over the years he had preserved it in secret. There was one other thing. It was an Indian carved wooden box, about two inches square, which Ella had given him after an important event had taken place. He opened it and inside, its tiny white rays and yellow disc dried and withered, but preserved and perfectly recognizable, was a daisy head. He took it out and held it in the palm of his hand. Somewhere, unless she had lost it, Ella had the other one. He would have to ask her.

Lee sat in the dark attic, with the weak light of the torch shining on the daisy head resting in the palm of his hand.

Honora knelt in the peace of the empty church, hearing only the sounds of the hail on the roof and the creaking of the hassock on which the priest knelt. She allowed her mind to range unfettered over vivid images of her dreamside experiences.

The memories flooded her with a sweet intensity. She felt the anxiety and the sheer pleasure that came with the control of dreamside. She felt the body's dreamside ache, a lust more physically acute than anything felt in the material, waking world. But she also remembered the fear, the brooding undertow beneath the earth and water and waxy sun of dreamside.

They were inseparable, this pleasure and this fear. Never before had she felt them so strongly. It was like a live thing inside her. She had called it from dreamside, the essence of dreamside, reforming, shape-shifting, soul-sucking, predatory, sloughing off one skin like a serpent, taking on new colors, all-devouring, breaking her down, covering her over with warm soil, reconstituting her, like a death without dying until buried over she became spice for the earth's pleasure. This was the thing the priest would take from her. This was the sin she could surrender to him.

She wanted purification. The priest would take her confusion and sin and guilt and doubt, and dissolve it. She felt it slip from her to him, memories that melted as they transposed themselves, her mind drained of all thoughts of lucid dream incarnations.

She opened her eyes. The priest had stopped praying and was looking at her. He was shocked. She knew instinctively that he'd had a taste of it, had peered over the edge and drawn back. He was unable to take it from her. What should have been dissolved between them had been arrested. Now bitterness hung on the air. His hands were trembling.

"You felt it!" said Honora. The priest failed to answer.

In despair she looked up at the plaster statue of the Virgin. The figure hanging over her swelled as she looked at it, and pulsed. This pulsing was the beating of her own heart. She desperately wanted release. It was all wrong. The priest couldn't help her. She looked at the figure of the plaster Virgin; at the flecks of skin-colored paint, faded with age to grey. Over how many failed confessions had this flaking plaster Virgin presided? How many prayers had dropped short?

Honora wanted to cry for her childhood. She wanted to cry for every Sunday School and for every mass she had attended, in their own way like lucid dreams—the invocation of hopes and the forfending of horrors. Her eyes were wet. As she looked up the Virgin stirred. There was a rustle of her blue robe and Honora was sure she heard her sigh. A whiff of decay hung on the air.

She sobbed and closed her eyes. Her memory fanned out across her faith; it was like watching the fragments of a shattered mirror reassembling: light streaming through stained glass; pungent smells of incense; votive candles flickering out; Latin words; all competing for her attention. She opened her eyes again, and this time the Virgin moved. Her eyes flicked open, and she struggled to speak. She saw her shiver, saw that she was real flesh, that her tears were wet and flowed and were an agony to her.

But her sobs turned to gasps as the figure began to change. She was appalled as it transformed, slowly, painfully, to the figure of the little girl. The girl swinging on the gate at home, the girl who would never leave her alone. The incarnation of Honora's sin. She felt dizzy, dislocated; a sick wave of fear rolled over her.

She felt something inside herself fall away. The girl fixed her with an unbroken gaze as she descended, glimmering faintly in the shadows of the church, moving slowly towards her, arms outstretched. The air turned cold: Honora could see her own breath icing over in front of her.

She was paralyzed. The girl was moving towards her, about to touch her. A blast of cold air passed from her. Her hands seemed cracked with the bitter cold and Honora shrank back from the diseased touch. The girl mouthed silent words. HERE I AM LORD; HERE I AM. As the girl drew close, Honora's screams echoed around the vaults.

The figure had changed again, had transformed back into the image of the Virgin, but this time more terrible, its body twisted and distorted with agony, wounds blistering and cracking on the painted flesh, open sores glistening and bleeding, its face contorted in a silent scream. The statue swayed, and came toppling down on top of her, the plaster Virgin shattering into fragments as it struck the hard floor of the church.

Ella entered the church to find the priest trying to drag the sobbing Honora away from the debris.

FIVE

"I'm afraid you are rather a careless dreamer,"
said Bertie resentfully
—Saki

Ella closed the bedroom door quietly behind her. "She's sleeping," she whispered to Lee, and they went through to the lounge.

"The priest helped me to get her to the car. Not exactly good in a crisis, that one. In fact he was in a terrible state. He seemed more concerned about his statue."

"Honora had actually pulled it down on top of her?"

"That's what it looked like, though she denies it."

"It's crazy. What did she tell you?"

"Very little. But whatever it was, the priest saw it too. He was in a state of shock. He couldn't—or wouldn't—tell me anything about it. He just wanted us out of there. But it was obvious to me that he was just as shaken up as she was." She sighed. "I don't say that I go along with it . . . but Honora is convinced that it's something from dreamside. A demon or a ghost or something . . ."

"Oh for Christ's sake Ella . . ."

"Lee, Honora thinks that her . . . *child* . . . has found a way to come through from dreamside."

"And you think it could be real."

She didn't have to answer. Lee looked very tired. He thought about the box in his attic.

A moan from Honora sent them scuttling along to the bedroom. She was sitting bolt upright. "Am I awake now?"

"Have you been dreaming the *repeater?*" asked Ella.

"Several times."

"This is awake."

"I wish I could believe you."

"Lee; give her a book."

Lee found a paperback. Honora turned the pages and read the opening lines:

> *The flood had made, the wind was calm, and being bound down the river, the only thing for it was to come to and wait for the turn of the tide.*

It read the same second time around.

"Somehow I still don't trust that," said Honora.

"Why don't you go back to sleep," coaxed Ella. "You look like you need it."

"I'm not going back to sleep!" Honora shouted.

"OK. Listen; I've got another idea."

"Whatever it is," Lee said to Honora, "you say no, and I'll say no."

"Agreed."

Ella bristled. "Why the hell do you both think we're here? Why am I here? Why are you here? Are we just renewing old friendships or what? Do I have to remind you that we're in some kind of crisis? I don't know about you two, but I don't want to spend the rest of my fucking life frightened to go to sleep! I want to end it!" She walked out of the room, slamming the door behind her.

"She's right isn't she?" Honora muttered.

"She's always right. One way or another."

Lee found Ella outside in the garden. He had stocked it with tall flowering plants. In summer it would be a paint box of delphiniums, snapdragons, foxgloves and flags growing up beside the red-brick wall. Along the top of the wall ran an untidy row of blue coping stones which only habit kept in place. In one corner of the garden was a trellis overburdened by a rampant growth of honeysuckle. In another corner, staked against the wall, was an ornamental tree.

She stood with her back to him, fingering the tiny pink matchheads of budding flowers. Lee came up softly behind her.

"Cherry blossom," she said. "I didn't even know it was here. It's getting ready to flare."

"I planted it years ago. To remind me of someone. But now it's pulling up the wall." He pointed at the base of the wall where the bricks, buckled by the tree's roots, pressed in towards the garden. "All it needs is a good push. Let's hear the plan."

"You won't like it."

"Can it be worse than the business in the church?"

"It concerns Brad Cousins."

"It's worse."

"Hear me out."

"I don't like it already. Neither will Honora."

"We've got to do something."

Ella stepped onto a brick protruding from the broken wall. She hoisted herself up and hooked her elbows over the row of coping stones. Lee stood behind her. "You'll have the wall down on us."

Ella didn't reply. She was looking at something on the other side. In the waste ground stood the girl she'd seen that morning, and had followed into the church.

She's bringing this on us, she thought.

She looked up at Ella and mouthed painful, silent words. They were visible, as if painted on the air. The same words: *help me help me help me*.

"What is it?" said Lee, sensing something.

"Nothing. Lift me down."

"Are you all right?" Lee lifted her down. He looked at her quizzically, before hoisting himself onto the wall, to see what had startled her.

"There's nothing there!" he said.

"No. Let's go indoors. I'm cold."

"Lee," she said when they were inside, "you've seen something of Honora's condition. She's not insane, though you may think *you* are before this thing is through. And she's only the first, she's not going to be the only one. We're all in danger. Something has started."

"What has started?"

"I just feel it. And it's coming to us all. How is your dreaming lately?"

"Every night a fight."

"To stay away from there?"

"To stay away. I'm afraid more than anything of going to sleep."

"And the repeaters?"

"Worse than ever."

"Then you do know of the danger. All of those dreamside dangers, they're coming home to roost. Only here, while we're awake. We can't hold out for ever. It's got to be resolved."

"But how?"

"I don't know. All I've got is ideas. But I'm not going to hide my

head and pretend it's not happening. And you've got to be strong."
She held on to his sleeves. "If you fall, we all will."

"What?" said Lee. "Why me?"

"It's true. You're the solid one."

But he knew she meant stolid. He also knew that it was she who
was the strongest one. She was going to have to carry three others.
She was just trying to give him some of her strength. He looked at her
and knew that if she commanded, he would try to realign the planets.

"Let's hear the plan."

"It's not going to be easy. We've got to take another walk on
dreamside, but this time with Brad and Honora. Together we have
to bury whatever it is that's out there."

"Or whatever it is that's in there. I'd say you've got about a fifty
percent resistance to that dreamside walk taking place."

"So long as it's no more than fifty per cent."

"I said I'll do it, and I meant it."

"Firstly there's Honora. You've got the influence. I know it.
She's always harbored a lot of feeling for you. You'll have to persuade her. She'll do it. She's got a much more acute sense than you of
the danger, and she's running out of energy. She's been fighting it for
longer. Make it clear she either does this thing once and for all or she
lives with it for ever. Tell her. Hold her hand. You might even have
to sleep with her."

"I hope you're joking, Ella."

"Push her hard. You can bring her to it, whereas I know I can't.
I know she'll come. You'll have room to maneuver. I'll be away
working on Brad."

"Will you be sleeping with him?"

"Only with my space suit on, after what you told me. You worry
about your own score. You can't bring Brad along; Honora certainly
wouldn't want to try; that leaves me. I'm going to have to bring him,
across my shoulder if necessary. I'm calculating on him being in the
same condition as Honora. If he is, I'll throw him a line and he'll

grab it. I'll go tomorrow, early. I figure we don't have a lot of time before something bad happens to one of us, and I want to be gone before Honora wakes up. I'll have Brad with me in under forty-eight hours or not at all. I'll phone to let you know. And you know where to meet us."

"Yes. I know where to meet you."

"I'll also need to take some things of yours with me."

"Take anything, Ella. You led me into this. You might as well lead me out."

"*I* led you in?"

"I never told you. All those years ago. I only ever went to that first dream meeting because of you. I stood behind you in a shadowy corridor, feeling horny, and I overheard you say you were going to the meeting. So I went. I never expected the rest."

"None of us expected the rest. Now let me tell you something about that first meeting. If you hadn't stood next to me in that corridor, and I hadn't spoken so loudly to make sure that you'd hear . . . That's made you look serious! Now kiss me; because it helps."

S I X

"I am real," said Alice, and began to cry
—Lewis Carroll

The next morning Ella was far away before Lee woke up for the third time, with a frightened start. Each false awakening was like breaking through a thin shell which would fragment and fall away only to reveal another one. This time it occurred to him to get out of bed and pick up a book. He let it fall open, read a paragraph twice and was relieved to find that it didn't change.

Honora found him in the kitchen. He was muttering over broken eggs. "You're awake," he said. "Any repeaters?" By now it was almost like saying good morning. You heard the sentiment but not the words.

"Lots. Where's Ella?" Honora looked better. She had color in her cheeks and her hair tumbled free over her shoulders.

"Gone to collect something." He would have to tell her later. Ella had told him to win her confidence, to get her to take that dreamside walk. How he was supposed to do that was anybody's guess.

He was still thinking about the episode in the church, and of his perspex shrine lying in a box in the attic. He could no longer pretend that Honora's problems didn't concern him, or that he was in any way outside of events. His rational objections had already dissolved, and he had been forced to recognize the seriousness of Ella's mission.

"Where did you say Ella had gone?" Honora said over breakfast.

"She had to go out to get something."

"What, exactly?"

This time he looked her deep in the eye before lying through his teeth. "She didn't say."

Being alone in the house with Honora made Lee feel on edge. He wasn't entirely certain what was creating the tension, but she clouded the air. It disturbed him. He cleared the dishes and busied himself at the sink. Honora hovered uncomfortably behind him for a moment before going through to the lounge. Then some movement outside the kitchen window caught Lee's eye.

"Wonder what she wants here?" he said aloud. He went outside, leaving the kitchen door open. Cold air fanned the house. Honora, who had also seen the girl, waited breathlessly in the lounge.

Lee wandered back. "Gone," he said, shutting the door behind him. "A kid. Sad little mouse, blue with cold. She looked at me as though she wanted something."

Honora said nothing.

Lee returned to the sink. Persuading Honora was not going to be easy. She would rather be lowered into a pit of snakes than meet up with Brad Cousins again, on dreamside or anywhere else. As for winning her confidence, Lee was out of practice at getting close to people. Nevertheless, at some point he would be obliged to steer the discussion around to Brad.

Lee plunged his arm into the hot water and took a plate. He heard the *ping!* and felt it split as he lifted it out. The hot water had broken it.

A hairline crack appeared in the center, spreading jaggedly both up towards the rim and down to his wrist. But then the crack extended itself at both ends simultaneously: at the top of the plate the crack skipped from the plate to rip at the plastic bowl, releasing a tide of foaming water. Then with a groan of tearing metal it wrenched apart the stainless steel sink itself, water gushing through the breach in the basin. At the other end of the plate the crack swept along the lifeline of the palm of Lee's hand. Skin cells popped and unzipped bloodily, following the curve of a vein in his forearm, marking its progress with a gory, congealed butcher's gash.

Lee was rooted. He let out a tiny gasp. Then he jumped backwards and dashed the plate to the floor where it shattered into minute fragments. The crack breaching the sink repaired itself and closed up instantly. The gash in his hand and arm healed.

Honora came running. Lee was staring at the palm of his hand. Honora took it as if she was looking for a burn, but she had already guessed part of the truth. The kitchen floor was awash with water.

"What happened?"

"I don't know!" said Lee. He was still looking for the phantom gash. "What *was* it? Did that really happen to me? It was like a . . . like a memory flash from dreamside. An elemental. Oh God!"

"Come through to the other room," said Honora.

"Are we awake? Or are we sleeping?"

Honora had already experienced these invasions into daytime. Lee hadn't, and was deeply shocked.

"We're awake. This has happened before."

"Often?"

"No, not often. But more frequently than we'd like."

"But the book . . . the acid test. I did it this morning."

"You can't trust it any more. The old rules are broken."

"God, I'm still shaking. I was being torn apart!"

Honora was still holding his hand. She leaned forward and kissed it lightly.

"What was that for?"

"That was for you." Her eyes were the blue of a lake.

"Honora, did you never meet anyone, after you left the university I mean. Did you never want to?"

"My one experience of men was enough."

"Are you going to blame everyone for that?"

"I don't know. After it all happened I went into hiding, and that became a habit."

"Did you never think that the reason for all of this might be that you were hiding, I mean repressing things."

"You've all got your boxed theories, haven't you? Ella's theory was Religious Guilt. Yours is Sexual Frustration. At bottom, neither of you wants to admit that there's the dream, the whole dream and nothing but the dream. So you try to put the problem on to me."

"That's not fair . . ."

"Come on. It's going to take more than a bit of pop psychology to clear the rats out of this cellar."

"Don't misunderstand me, Honora. I wasn't suggesting that we . . ."

"Well, I could do worse. Look at you, you're easily shocked! And why not anyway? Things could easily have been different."

"What do you mean?"

"Oh . . . let it go."

"You mean it could have been you and me instead of Ella and me."

"Oh no, not really. Ella was always the bright sparkle on the water. She made me feel like I was standing in the shade. I always admired her and felt a little jealous at the same time."

"I can't imagine you as the jealous type. What was there to be jealous of anyway?"

"Well, she had you for one thing."

"Oh come on Honora, be serious."

"No, really, it's true. I liked the way you could sit back from a situation, when others argued; you always seemed to have . . . reserves."

"You're mistaking the absence of ideas for reserves; I just didn't have anything to contribute. I always thought: go which way the wind blows."

"That's not such a bad philosophy, is it?"

"You're wrong about that. I've lived all my life in a draft!"

"Oh go on. Don't put yourself down."

Lee thought how easily indeed it might have been different. There was a moment back there, years ago, in the shadow of a doorway somewhere, between Honora and himself. But the moment had been distracted by a sparkle on the water, when Ella had dropped back and had steered him by the elbow down a different path.

Lee put his hand into the nest of brown curls tied back above Honora's neck, and felt them slide over his fingers like cool, live things. But when he tried to draw her to him, she resisted.

"Too late for all that," she said.

"Yes, but I'm going to kiss you anyway."

This time she consented. She put her mouth on his, and her tongue flicked at his mouth. Through half-closed eyes, he saw her nut-brown curls tumbling free and twisting towards him. He thought of Ella's words before she left, about sleeping with Honora, and he knew that Ella had seen this, hadn't been joking. Or maybe he credited Ella with too much vision, maybe she had just been afraid of this happening. But he closed his eyes and all thoughts of Ella were subsumed in the honeyed kiss. Honora's lips were sweet and her inexperience excited him. She smelled of the freshly falling rain.

Then he opened his eyes and he saw not Honora's face, but a child's. A girl child's, the color and texture of white candle-wax; the sick, unhealthy face of the child who had eyed him that very morning from the bottom of his garden.

And now he saw not the waving curls of Honora's hair, but a writhing, spitting nest of vipers. Her eyes had turned the dull yellow-gold of a venomous serpent. He tried to pull back, but his tongue petrified in her mouth and the saliva on their lips became a glue which bonded them. Tearing himself away was the agony of lips lacerating in strips of flesh. He gasped and flung himself backwards, crashing into the table and shattering the glass cabinet in the corner of the room.

"What is it? What happened?" cried Honora, getting up to help him.

"No! No! Don't touch me!"

The vision had already disappeared. All he could see now was Honora's helpless and horrified expression, her arms lifted towards him, a trace of blood on her mouth. But he couldn't let her near him.

S E V E N

I have observed that in some individuals, the high-
est aspirations are for no more than the sovereignty
of dreams above fantasies. In seeking to define this
condition we might also ask whether there might
return some form of psychological retribution for
the crime of living so vaguely.
—L. P. Burns

A peculiar instinct guided Ella, offering soundings of what was swimming in the depths around her, what to avoid, where to go next. She charted her course by this intuitive sensory apparatus, and she was rarely wrong.

Wrapped in her fleece-lined flying jacket she accelerated the Midget down the fast lane. The motorway was choked in its own stratosphere of exhaust fumes. Her split-leather holdall lay on the passenger seat, stuffed with Lee's possessions. Though her foot was firmly pressed on the accelerator, she felt decidedly less than confident.

Her sonar instinct couldn't be held responsible for the fact that Ella, knowing with uncanny prescience where trouble or difficulty lay, would often head straight for it. Nature always seemed to volunteer her to be the one to jump through hoops of fire; though to her credit she never asked anyone to take responsibility for it but herself. She was committed to her current course of action. There was no going back.

Driving south, she passed a car which had broken down on the hard shoulder. Shortly after, she was overtaken by a dirty white estate car piled high with luggage. A kid with a sickly, lop-sided grin made faces and waved at her through the rear window as it sped by. The kid made her think of Brad Cousins.

She had been right about Honora and the Church. What had happened between Honora and the priest had happened precisely because Ella was right, even if the event had failed to resolve things. Had she been wrong, Honora would have walked away with a rosary and a soothed conscience, but with their group problem unsolved. Now, she knew, she was right about having to bring them all together. It was unfortunate to be always right.

Before she did anything else, she and Brad had some business to sort out, something to get straight. Then Brad would come. She would make him come. From Lee's description of Brad's physical state she didn't need to guess at his psychological condition. Of the four, only Lee seemed to be standing up to the increasing pressure, the cracks which had begun to appear in the fabric of reality itself, the invasions from dreamside. She hadn't mentioned her own recent experiences— better to keep the lid screwed down tight. If he had so far managed to stay clear of the frightening distortions that had crept up on her over the last few days, then that could become a source of strength.

Ella herself had been suffering the horrors of these attacks for some time, without saying anything to Lee. She had survived them only with the intellectual effort of the reversal techniques they had all learned on dreamside, sometimes with effect, sometimes with-out. Lee had had no idea of what she had seen over his garden wall the previous afternoon. She had said nothing because she wanted to shield him from what was bearing down on the rest of them. He was the one with the slightest sense of the real danger.

As for the others, Honora was in a wildly unstable condition. Her encounter with the priest showed that she was wired up to all kinds of energies. But Ella calculated that Brad was the weakest of them all. Brad had been the strongest, most powerful dreamer; con-sequently those energies he had spent so freely on dreamside would now be making their claims on him, with interest. He would be the most susceptible to these attacks. Which is why he would now, in all probability, be lying drunk somewhere.

Ella sailed past a car which had broken down on the hard shoulder. Shortly after, the Midget was overtaken by a dirty white estate car packed full of luggage, a child with a lop-sided grin making faces at her and waving through the back window as it went by.

Didn't that just happen, back there? The sense of *déjà vu* was acute and powerful, but she credited the event to tiredness and dismissed it. She was more concerned about the impending encounter with Brad. If Lee's accounts were not exaggerated, she might be lucky to find him conscious when she arrived. On the other hand, Lee had been certain that Brad wouldn't be going anywhere. Ella would have a captive audience.

For the third time Ella passed a car which had broken down on the hard shoulder, but now she noticed the driver in the act of opening the door and climbing from his seat. She put her foot down hard, but sure enough, was overtaken by the grubby estate car complete with the manic child grinning back at her through the rear window. The landscape around the motorway went on unchanged for miles, a deep swath through the countryside, lacking any distinctive landmark. Ella had lost all sense of where she was. She kept her foot hard down.

For some days she had struggled against hallucinations and distortions. She knew how to suppress the initial rising panic, signalled by a familiar but unidentified metallic taste in the mouth. But this was different, as indeed they always were. She passed the stranded roadside car yet again, and helplessly, with a deep sickening recognition, watched the sequence regenerate itself as the estate car sped past her.

This time she identified the malevolent face in the back of the car. She had seen it before, and more than once. She could identify every sick feature of that girl's face; just as she knew exactly who the girl was. The air was seeded with something colorless, odorless, tasteless, but yet dense and oppressive. She knew it was in control of the loop in which she was trapped, controlling events. Even now it regulated the flow of traffic, closing it up to block her from moving into the inside lane. She was being obstructed from pulling over, prevented from moving out of the loop.

Ella drove on. In the distance she saw the stranded motor coming up on the left-hand side. She slowed and indicated to pull in, but the procession of traffic on the inside lane had squeezed together. No one would give way. She sailed past the car parked on the hard shoulder, helplessly watching the rest of the sequence play itself out.

Again she saw the stranded car on the left. Again she slowed and signalled to move in, and again no one would allow her the space. She gripped the wheel and turned recklessly into the car abreast of her. There was a blast of horns and a shrieking of tires as she squeezed the Midget into a silhouette's space between two chrome fenders, a space so narrow it wouldn't have admitted a playing card. Miraculously, she made it, skidding and braking on the hard shoulder, scraping the side of the Midget along the crash barriers, stopping bumper to bumper behind the car which had broken down.

The driver was already climbing out of his seat. He came, opened Ella's passenger door, and said: "That was close."

Ella, still trembling, lit a cigarette.

She was too shocked to respond, or to look up at the man standing over her. She got an impression of an elderly figure in a long beige raincoat and smartly polished brown shoes. She knew exactly who it was.

Ella heard his voice as if from a great distance. "I had faith that you would stop. Faith will move mountains, but it won't drive the internal combustion engine."

She pulled harder on her cigarette as she felt the man climbing into her passenger seat. She could only manage a whisper. "Oh God; am I dreaming?"

"Don't be afraid. You needed me." It was almost the same gentle, reassuring voice which Professor Burns had used to guide them through their early experiments with lucid dreaming. Burns put his hand on Ella's arm. His grip was warm, but she shivered.

"Help us, Professor."

"Drive a little, Ella."

Rigid with fear, she started the motor and rolled the car back on to the motorway. It was easier than having to look Burns in the eye. She drove slowly, blindly, thinking: How do we wake up? How?

It was a long time before Burns spoke. "You are in danger, Ella. Serious danger. All four of you. You stayed too long on dreamside. You have left a terrible need there, and it calls you back. And it will have you back. Your minds are unravelling. Even now it's winding you in." Burns was agitated.

"But what can be done? What can we do?"

Burns paused. Ella couldn't look at him. Her eyes settled instead upon his hands, which he was twisting together. "Undo what was done."

"How? How can you undo what isn't there?"

"How did it come to be? Dismiss it in the same way. This is the best help I can give you. But beware. This is the danger of dreamside: those who stay too long may never be allowed back. All four of you have stayed too long."

The professor pressed his hands together, as if in prayer. Then he looked nervously over his shoulder at the road behind.

"Are you cold, Professor?"

"Oh yes, cold. Always cold. Stop the car. I will get out. Then you must think that this meeting never really happened."

Ella coasted to a stop on the hard shoulder. Burns got out and closed the door. Nothing more was said. She steered back onto the motorway. Through the rear-view mirror she could see him staring after her. Then she blinked, and saw the girl gazing at her from the spot where he had stood. The figure of the girl diminished in the distance.

Ella was becoming unstuck. So many overwhelming things were happening she could only try to move with the flow. The old forms had to be abandoned. She had to learn new, simpler rules for existing: *can I feel it* / *does it stop me?* Who was that in the car with her a moment ago? The professor? The girl? Or neither, just phantoms gathering out of a zone of madness they had come to call *the dreamside*.

She had to keep herself together long enough to get Brad back to the others. That was the only important thing now. She continued her journey braced against further horrors. Three hours later she stopped the car outside an isolated cottage.

Lee had told her to look out for two cottages, but all she could see was this one and the charred and blackened shell of another burned-down building near by. The roof had gone and a side wall had fallen in. At the holes where window and door frames had all been burned out, the stone was charred with soot patches like great black rags hung upside-down. Ella thought she could still detect the smell of charred wood in the air.

Fixed beside the door of the remaining cottage, however, was a split wooden plaque bearing the name Elderwine, just as Lee had described. Ella walked right in.

In the first room she entered, she saw Brad Cousins in yellowing underclothes, lounging on an old sofa. His feet were drawn up beneath him, and he was blowing smoke at the ceiling.

"I've been waiting for you," he said.

"You're the second person today," said Ella.

E I G H T

MERCY: *I was a-dreaming that I sat all alone in a*
solitary place and was bemoaning of the hardness
of my heart
—John Bunyan

"Is this the best you can do?" Ella, in her WWII flying jacket, stood framed in the shadowy doorway. She looked to Brad like a modern Valkyrie, or some other messenger of the gods, come to peck at his liver.

"You look great," he said, "the crow's feet under your eyes give you character, though your breasts have sagged. Also your jaw has slackened off, which has lifted the venom sacs from under your lip. Really, you look better. Where did you land the Spitfire?"

"I could have landed a small aircraft in your mouth. That hasn't changed."

"Give me one of those godawful poseur's cigarettes you always smoke."

Ella swept newspapers and empty brown ale bottles from a chair on to the floor. She inspected the seat closely before deciding to sit. Expertly hand-rolling one of her liquorice-paper cigarettes, she tossed it to Brad. "This place makes me want to puke."

"Well, we didn't know the princess was coming."

"Thought you said you were expecting me?"

"The servants are away this week."

"You're almost coherent—I'm surprised. That must mean something's wrong. I thought you'd be drunk."

"Dear old Ella; she's very clever. And she'd fuck anyone for fourpence."

Ella only shrugged. "You can do better than that, a man of your bile."

"Have you really come to peck at my liver?"

"Don't be obscure."

"Never mind. Never you mind, me old princess." He hoisted himself up off the sofa, swaying slightly as he came forward and stood over her, uncomfortably close in his filthy T-shirt and yellow-stained underpants. Lee's graphic descriptions hadn't been exaggerated. His hair was matted and his stubbled chin was stained by something saffron colored he must have eaten recently. The smell of his unwashed body turned Ella's stomach.

He had a bad look in his eye as he stood provocatively near, arms dangling at his side, puffing on his cigarette, waiting for some kind of reaction. She wanted to tell him that he smelled like the carcass of something washed up and rotting on a beach. She thought better of it, taking a pull on her own cigarette and meeting his eyes, but as if with infinite patience. It was always possible he might just smash her in the face.

He snapped his fingers loudly and turned away to find his bottle. "Do you want a drink me old princess me old duchess me old empress? Do you?"

"Oh it's a cocktail bar! And I thought I was in a hovel! I'll pass, but don't let me stop you from getting any further out of focus."

Brad slumped back on the couch with his whisky. "How's your boyfriend? He paid me a courtesy call recently—we go back a long way you know—he wanted me to join his golf club. Had to disappoint him. Don't even know why he came. And a couple of weeks later, here you are. Imagine."

"Imagine. One more and we'd have the full set."

Brad scowled. "But what could Ella want with me, eh? What could the old harpy want with Brad?"

"Still pretending, are we Brad?"

"Pretending? Pretending what?"

"Pretending we're not pretending."

"Gibberish. With a capital *ish*."

"Why did you call us, Brad?"

He looked at Ella with contempt. "You *what?*"

"You called us."

"Talk shit."

"I always could out-guess you, Brad. You never liked that, did you? Now that I see you, I'm more certain than ever it was you."

"You don't come here to lecture me; I know what you are. You're dirt. You're diseased! Unhinged!"

Ella went over to Brad and kneeled down beside the sofa. She put her hand into his matted hair. "You're still a boy, aren't you Brad? A big boy, but still a boy."

"Piss off! Get the fuck out of here!" But he made no attempt to pull back from her.

"You know, Brad, for a long time I thought it was Honora, going back there, shrouded in guilt. But it was you, wasn't it? You started it again. We were all asleep, for years; then you went back there, and you needed us, so you woke us all up. Didn't you, Brad? You called us."

"Just go would you? Just go." Something in Brad's voice had fractured.

"Here I am, Brad."

"No."

"You have to tell me, Brad. You have to."

"No!"

"It can't go on. You know it. You have to tell me."

Brad looked at her. She had never seen such desperation. "She's out there, Ella."

"Who?"

"She's out there. She's hungry."

"Who's out there? Honora?"

"No no no no no. Not her. *She*."

"But who is she? You must tell me."

"Out *there*. She's hungry. She wants to eat me . . . the little girl."

"How can a little girl hurt you, Brad?"

"She's not a little girl. Just pretending. Disguised. She hates me. She wants to eat me. Stop looking at me like that." Brad buried his head in the sofa. "Stop it!"

"Why can't I look at you?"

"Because I'm disgusting. I'm a leper. Don't look at me, Ella."

Ella pulled Brad to her, and cradled his head in her lap, stroking his filthy, matted hair as he cried. It was an hour before his sobbing subsided.

They were standing in the kitchen. "When did you sleep last?"

Ella had salvaged and scoured four of Brad's biggest saucepans. She had filled them with water and they were heating on the front and back plates of the filthy electric cooker. The water began to bubble.

"I haven't slept for three days and nights. I'm too scared to sleep."

"Like the rest of us then. Well? Are you going to bring it in?"

Brad shuffled uncomfortably. "Come on, do it," said Ella.

Brad went out of the back door and returned clumsily maneuvering an old tin bath. "Where shall I put it?" he asked pathetically. Ella wiped the tin bath with a damp rag until she was satisfied that it was as clean as she was going to get it, then poured in the hot water. It amounted to about three inches in the bottom of the bath.

This was topped up with cold water, and the four saucepans were immediately refilled and set to boil.

"What are you waiting for?" she said. "I'm certainly not going to undress you."

Brad stared back at her, and eventually began fumbling with his underclothes. Undressed, he climbed into the bath and drew his knees up around him. "It's not very warm," he said sulkily.

Ella produced her leather holdall, from which she withdrew soap, sponge, scrubbing brush, towels, razors, shaving brush, shaving soap, scissors, combs, shampoo, deodorants and cologne. She lined them up on the kitchen table like a surgeon's equipment. Then she set to work, vigorously scrubbing Brad's neck and shoulders.

"Steady!" shouted Brad.

Ella didn't ease up. "It's disgusting."

"You're enjoying this, aren't you!"

"It's what I live for."

She splashed soapy water over his head, and drew the line at washing him below the waist.

"You would have, once."

"Never; and don't forget it." She tossed a jug of cold water over his head by way of emphasis.

The water turned black. She refilled the bath with more hot water from the stove, reheating pans all the time. After washing his hair, she proceeded to cut it none too carefully, telling him that it was fashionable to look like someone from a thirties soup kitchen. He said he doubted it.

"I met someone on the way down here," said Ella as she snipped recklessly close to Brad's ears. "I gave him a lift. He gave me some advice before he got out of the car. He said . . ."

"Watch my ear for chrissake!"

"Sorry . . . He said we should undo what was done."

"Big help."

"Do you know what he meant?"

"Christ! Watch my ears will you! That was deliberate!"

"Sorry. This man—at least at first I thought he was a man, then I thought he might be just a phantom, from dreamside—was helping me. He was a friend. At least he seemed to be."

"Other things have happened."

Ella was careful to release only part of the story. If she mentioned the girl at this point, it would all be over. "That's the trouble. Not being able to tell the difference, I mean. That's why it's dangerous."

Brad just stared into the murky water which was turning cold around his genitals. He was pink with scrubbing. His ears were sore from clippings gone wide of the mark, deliberate or otherwise. He was beginning to feel sober and he was beginning to feel ridiculous. Ella whisked up a lather of shaving soap, sculpted it around his jaw and set in with the razor.

"I'm relieved you're doing this with us Brad. It's the only way."

"Did Honora agree to it?"

"She will."

"I don't see what good it can do."

"Just don't change your mind."

"Did you ever tell Lee about us?" he said suddenly.

She didn't stop shaving him. "There was nothing to tell."

"I mean about that one time. Us. On dreamside."

"It never happened, Brad. Not between you and me."

"I know different. We discussed it years ago; you denied it then."

"And I deny it now. Whatever dream you had that time, even if I was in it, I wasn't there."

"You can say that now." He flicked water from his eye.

"You're wrong."

"No, I'm not."

"Careful while I'm holding this razor. I'll say it again: I wasn't there."

Brad went to contradict her; but he saw a cold gleam in her eyes like a reflection of the razor she was wielding. It made him stop. It was so long ago even he couldn't pretend that the contours of truth hadn't folded a little. Lucid or otherwise, it was all dreaming. "I'm getting cold," he said.

Ella stood him up, poured another pan of cold water over his head and wrapped him in a towel. She gave him sweet-smelling lotions together with instructions for liberal use; and a complete set of clothes belonging to Lee. He disappeared from the kitchen to try them on.

When he returned, with his cropped hair combed back and the trouser cuffs and sleeves of the oversized suit turned up, Ella started giggling. Brad retreated angrily, slamming the door, refusing to come out again and threatening not to make the return journey to rejoin the others. But finally she got him into the car. He climbed into the passenger seat and sat with arms crossed and with head bowed.

"I need to tell the others we're on our way," said Ella.

She stopped the car at a telephone kiosk to make a progress report to Lee. Stepping out of the car, she had a second thought, and reached for the keys.

"What's that for?" Brad demanded. It was the first time he had spoken since leaving the cottage.

"Reflex."

"What's the matter with you? Do you think I'd drive off in the car or something?" He was angry.

"Relax. I'm just going to make one phone call."

"You're taking the keys anyway, I see!"

Inside the booth, and away from Brad for the first time in over six hours, she sighed deeply, leaning her head against the dial. Brad's behavior was still unpredictable, and he was in a highly suggestible state. So far he had followed, but if he was to have a change of heart she would never be able to bring him back again. If she could keep her own head clear she might do it. She was terrified by the idea of what might happen if he or she experienced an attack en route.

She carefully phoned Lee's number. When the answer came, it was Honora on the line, though her voice could hardly be made out. The line was full of interference, strange electronic chirpings, and innumerable unfathomable ghost conversations, as if a hundred other people were trying to claim the line. Ella put the receiver down and tried again, but got the same results.

"Phone's out of order," she told Brad, back in the car. "It'll have to wait."

Brad only stared sulkily ahead of him. "This car will never make it," he said.

Ella could sense two forces working in Brad. One surrendered him completely to her judgment, and with blind faith asked her to take charge and deliver him from his nightmares. The other was a palpable terror, growing so fast she could smell it on his breath: a fear both of facing the source of his horrors, and of facing his fellow dreamers with whom he had brought the living nightmare into being. This terror, she knew, was already telling him that in coming with her he had made a mistake; and his apprehension of that mistake was increasing with each mile of their journey.

It was beginning to get dark. At a service station half-way up the motorway she stopped and tried to phone again. She got no better results—a line awash with interference, busy with sounds like whispered conversations which changed as soon as you tried to listen in on them. When she returned to the car park, Brad was gone.

She found him in the reception area of the service station, hanging over an electronic arcade machine. A space patrol game. His hand fumbled with the joystick as he peered darkly into the kaleidoscope of shifting pin-lights behind the black glass.

"Time to go," said Ella.

"But I haven't beaten the invaders. The earth's in peril."

"You have to put some money in to do that."

"Oh . . . sure." He released the stick and followed her back to the car.

Shortly after she had turned off the motorway, Brad suddenly seemed to emerge from a daze. "I need a drink," he said.

"Brad; it would be a good idea if you stayed off the pop."

He gripped her wrist hard enough to make her stop the car. "I need a drink."

His eyes were almost crazy with fear and lack of sleep.

"Maybe you do. I'll find a pub."

She had to drive for a while along a winding and deserted country road. Dusk was slipping away quickly into darkness. She found a place with a dimly lit sign saying The Corn Man. It had the expectant hush of a pub just opened and too early for most customers. Brad marched up to the bar and ordered himself two large brandies, both of which he drank, leaving Ella to order herself a tonic water. He repeated his order, and the barmaid eyed him quizzically as she nudged his glass under the optic measure.

"Ease up," said Ella. "Lee will bring enough to keep you satisfied."

"Lee Lee Lee. Lee schmee."

Brad kept a hand on one of his brandy glasses, as if someone might want to take it away from him. Ella waited patiently, in silence. At length he got up. "Must take a leak," he said.

Ella sat nursing her tonic water until she realized that he wasn't coming back. She even stood outside the gents' toilets, calling to him, but she knew he wasn't in there. She returned to her car and sat behind the wheel, not knowing what to do. Half an hour had passed before he walked out of the shadow and climbed back in the passenger seat. She thought he had the smell of vomit on him.

"What are we waiting for?" he said.

N I N E

*It has been often remarked that a hen is only an
egg's way of making another egg*
—Samuel Butler

"I'm sure it was Ella." Honora didn't sound at all sure.

"What did she say?"

"I didn't hear anything. She sounded like she was phoning from another planet. I couldn't make her out."

Lee hadn't quite recovered from his vision of Honora as a Gorgon, his second attack of elementals within the space of minutes. For the moment he was less concerned with Ella's difficulties than with his own. He hadn't drawn breath to consider what might have happened between Honora and himself if the hallucination hadn't intervened. What's more, he was no closer to having explained Ella's absence.

"Where would she be phoning from?"

"She wouldn't be too far away."

"Why won't you tell me where she's gone? Why won't you answer me?"

Lee was running short of escape lines and changes of subject. He actually contemplated faking another attack of writhing snakes in order to divert her questions. A deep intuition told him not to play games.

Fortunately Honora backed off. He tried to distract himself by shuffling playing cards on the coffee table, pretending to deal rounds of patience, but lacked concentration. Still shaking from that last attack, he felt sick to his stomach.

His anxiety was exacerbated by Honora, who gave him the jitters simply by sitting still with her hands gently clasped in an attitude of such perfect serenity that it could not fail to betray the deep agitation within. Worse, it had dawned on Lee that Honora had become aware, either by intuition or by the simple application of common sense, that Ella had gone to recruit Brad Cousins into her latest scheme. A disconcerting feeling came over him. He felt, irrationally, that he was unwittingly projecting mental pictures to Honora, or that she had found some ghoulish means of bleeding him of information.

It was difficult enough being subject to these random mental distortions without fearing that there was some kind of telepathy going on. It could be another overspill from dreamside, the residual thoughtspeak of dreamside. Anyway, it was happening. And when Lee admitted this, he felt a corresponding wave in Honora. They sat up and looked at each other, and there was a dovetailing of insight. He knew she knew, and she knew he knew she knew, and so it went, back into infinite space.

Lee continued to turn cards, gnawed at by visions of his earlier hallucination.

Honora stepped over to the window, peering out at the dusk. She snatched the curtains closed.

"Shall I tell your future?" she said suddenly. "From the cards. Shall I?"

"I don't want to know it under the circumstances."

"You don't have to believe it!"

"That's what I told myself the other night. I don't have to believe in the power of dreaming. I told myself several times, but it didn't help."

"Nonsense. Give me the cards." Honora knelt alongside the coffee table and gathered up the pack. Lee sat back, putting a respectful distance between himself and any possible repeat hallucination. Briefly shuffling the cards, Honora started placing them across each other on the table, intoning as she turned them up. "This crowns you, this crosses you, this circles you; this is beneath you and this is behind you; this speaks for you, this will deceive you, this will defend you, and this is all before you."

Lee didn't get to see his future because the phone rang. This time he answered.

"It's Ella," he said. "Ella, you'll have to shout; I said you'll have to shout; I said . . . Jesus this is hopeless . . . I said I still can't hear you!"

Lee could just make out that it was Ella, but her message was lost in a flurry of static and signal interference. There was a wall of sound crackling from the earpiece. From the middle of it Ella's voice piped through, but was distant and stripped of tone and amplitude. Her voice had been reduced to the narrowest frequency, a single oscillation playing along a fine wire that could have been stretching half the length of the galaxy. Ella was there and he could hear her, but he couldn't identify a single word she was saying. The line seemed full of breathing and whisperings, and waves of static, all conspiring to crowd her out. Lee pressed his ear closer to the receiver.

"YOU'LL HAVE TO SHOUT, ELLA!" The electronic piping of her voice continued, sounding like the noise an electronic or mechanical bird might produce, against the unabated interference. "ELLA? WHAT IS IT YOU'RE SAYING?"

Lee felt his earlobe, pressed tight against the earpiece, start to get hot, then smart and sting. Then he felt a sharp sensation like a pin being inserted into the tender part of his ear. As he pulled the phone away from his head it jerked at him, as if his ear had become glued to the receiver. Pulling at it only produced a searing pain, like flesh tearing away in strips.

"Honora!" he shouted. This time he knew what was happening. Honora jumped to her feet.

But the stinging continued, until it felt like a razor cutting his ear, or something gripping him tightly like a pair of scissors. He tried to breathe deeply and control the hallucination, as he had done on dreamside many times, thinking in detail down the procession of events, smoothing back the sequence of the attack. Then he felt himself begin to panic as he felt out of control.

"There's something inside the phone!" Honora shouted.

Lee felt it now; and as he inched the receiver away from his head he could almost see at the periphery of his vision the dull gleam of yellow blades snapping and twisting and bringing blood to his ear. A black feathered head squeezed out of the earpiece, shaking frantically, eyes bulbous with fear, and he realized that what was tearing at his ear was not a razor, not scissors, but the sharp pecking beak of a bird. Honora screamed and stood over him, not knowing what to do to help. Lee wrenched the phone away from his head. The bird, large, the size of a blackbird, squeezed out of the earpiece, its wings flapping wildly as they came free, first one then the other, still pecking and cutting at Lee's bloodied ear in wild panic.

Dropping the phone and lashing out with his hand, Lee smashed it up and away over his head. The bird flew frantically around the room, disastrously, crashing into walls and thrashing against the window. Lee crumpled and retched and vomited. The bird swooped crazily, and flew into objects around the room. The black rag of its wings was magnified by the confinement of space, fanning them with ice-cold waves of air. Torn feathers came floating down around them, until at last Honora, screaming and crying, in utter desperation picked up the coffee table and hurled it through the central window. The glass shattered spectacularly, and the table fell back into the room. The bird flew out of the smashed window and away into the dusk outside.

Honora staggered over to where Lee lay on the floor. She hoisted him up by his waist. Breathing heavily she said, "Come on; you've got to get up; you've got to get up."

"It was real," he panted. "You saw it. It was real. It wasn't a hallucination at all." His ear was bloodied and torn.

"Of course I saw it. You must get up. It's time for us to go isn't it? Ella was trying to tell us it's time. They're both going to be there, aren't they?"

Lee nodded. He was beginning to understand why Ella had been in so much of a hurry.

"Get some overnight things; get some blankets and covers. I'll get the rest. Then get in the car."

They loaded up the car in silence. Then they drove away, dusk slipping into darkness, leaving the gaping hole of the smashed window in the empty house behind them.

A foul wind came up, assaulting the room they had left, like a raid made a few moments too late. It flapped the heavy curtains beside the broken window and flipped Honora's unread cards, dealing a new sequence, one darker and full of portents which only the wind could read.

T E N

*We may need to characterize and distinguish
respectively between the deceptions and distortions
of our desires; through the media of memory,
fantasy, neuroses, dreaming, and finally through
those unhinged kinds of love which themselves
spiral deeper and deeper into madness*
—L. P. Burns

Somewhere in the Brecon Beacons, guided in the moonless dark by an infrared confidence and a blueprint memory, Ella found her mark. It was the early hours of the morning. The Midget, engine knocking wildly, stalled outside the house on the exact spot where an old Morris Minor had stood one summer thirteen years ago. Ella had already jumped out, leaving Brad to stare moodily around him. The house stood empty.

"Thirteen years on," she said to Brad, "and still a holiday home for some overpaid academic who's probably been twice since we were here."

Brad got out of the car. He didn't begrudge anyone a single brick of the place. "How will we get in?" he said, in a voice that suggested. "Let's turn back."

Ella lifted the boot of her car. "You've got a narrow experience of life, Brad Cousins." She lifted a slender chisel and a hammer from the boot, and marched around to the rear of the house. Brad followed at a distance of five paces. She slotted the chisel between the upper and lower frame of a sash window, swung the hammer once, hard, and the window catch flew open. The window required only a light push, sliding up as if by hydraulic gears.

"Where did you learn that?"

"From a cigarette card. Go and fetch those things from the car."

Brad trotted off obediently as Ella climbed through the window. When he reappeared with Ella's bag, she had the back door open.

"No, don't switch on the lights. We don't want to attract attention. Anyway, it'll soon be light. Close the curtains and light some of these candles."

"Romantic," said Brad.

"You think so?"

"No."

With the candle flames flickering and darting long shadows across the room, they could see that the house had recently been renovated. Floorboards had been sanded, old cupboards replaced by units, and the enamel sink supplanted by one of stainless steel. They made coffee and played a nervous round of That-Wasn't-Here-Before.

"What time will the others come?"

"When they show up."

"Give me one of those ridiculous liquorice cigarettes, will you?"

Some time after three o'clock in the morning, a car pulled up outside the house. Ella went to the window and drew back a curtain. Then she opened the door.

"We got well lost," said Lee, "we've been driving in circles. Scary kind of circles." He gave Ella a special look.

So now Lee *was* getting a taste, Ella thought. Now he understands what's happening. "Don't tell me about it. You're here. Come inside, Honora."

"Is he in there?"

Ella nodded, and they walked through. Brad sat stiffly in a corner of the room. Lee was only mildly surprised to see him shaved, shorn and kitted out in one of his old suits. Honora simply erased his presence: he wasn't there. Brad might have flickered a glance in her direction, or maybe it was only the play of candlelight across his eyes.

Lee rubbed his hands with simulated gusto, paced the floor and chattered about making coffee and getting comfortable: anything to overlay the smoky bitterness in the room. Ella was wiser than Lee. She knew the exact nature of the ingredients that had to be brought together to bubble in the cauldron. Let them feel it, she thought, let them feel it.

Lee discovered what hard work it is to keep up conversation when three other people don't want to join in. He quickly ran out of counterfeit enthusiasm. The candles burned steadily, and the four sat silently, nursing empty coffee mugs, only their eyes reflecting the available light. Occasionally a flame would shiver in a draft, dispatching shadows across a wall and releasing a worm of black smoke.

"This is like a séance," said Lee. "Let's see if we can contact the living."

No one bothered to laugh. Lee was reminded of the early lucid dreaming seminars, where they would sit for twenty minutes in uncomfortable silence waiting for the professor to speak. He was about to wonder aloud what Burns would have made of their situation, but opted against unwise comment. Honora gazed down at the rug beneath her as if she saw something significant in its pattern, and it seemed to Lee that her silence was the deepest. Brad continued to find the far corner of the ceiling an image of satisfaction. Ella looked far too comfortable, and the corners of her mouth were turned up fractionally in what he thought was an incipiently malevolent smile.

That Ella was in charge was unquestionable. The other three had by now surrendered themselves to her. They all knew why they were here, but they were waiting for Ella to summon them to order. She seemed to have the power to draw something out of them, to distill something from the brooding silence. When Ella did speak, the others were steeled to listen.

"No one's in any mood for sleeping; and we all know why that is. In any event I'm wide awake, and the dawn will be up in an hour or two. Better save it for tomorrow night, when we will need to sleep. We have to take that walk together on dreamside." Ella paused for effect, and released a deep sigh.

"Tomorrow," she continued, "or rather when it gets light, we'll go and take a look at the lake. We'll just spend the day together, however much effort that takes. It's what Burns showed us. It worked before and it will work for us again. Tomorrow night we sleep, and we do it. Agreed?" Ella looked from person to person but all eyes were averted. "There can't be any stragglers."

"Ella," said Brad self-consciously, making a waving sign at his mouth.

"Sure," said Ella. "Lee, I hope you didn't forget Brad's medicine?"

"What?"

"Did you bring anything for him?"

"Oh sure," said Lee, glad to do something useful. He went out and returned with a half-empty bottle of whiskey. "Don't scowl at it; there's more in the car."

"Don't give him ideas," said Ella, but not before Brad had hooked back a good belt of Scotch.

Before the candles had burned down, the first grey light of the day leaked into the room. The dawn chorus was in song before they realized it, followed by a brighter light. Honora went round snuffing out candles, slowly, like a church acolyte. Ella watched her and was afraid for her. She had spent most of the night in complete silence, haunting everyone else with her inward stare. Now she stood poised over the last candle, thumb and forefinger moistened to nip out the flickering light, but arrested in the motion. She gazed steadily into the flame without blinking. It was as if her soul was a fine thread being unwound from a thick spool and pulled in toward the heart of the flame.

"Look at her," Ella whispered to Lee, "something is taking her, a little at a time."

"What is it?"

Ella shook her head. "Stop her."

Lee moved up behind Honora, gently reaching over her shoulder to nip out the candle flame. She seemed to wake up.

"Have I been sleeping?" she asked.

Lee looked over at Ella, but they said nothing. Then Ella pulled back the curtains, looked up at the sky and pronounced that it was going to be a fine day. Brad snorted.

"We'll go for a walk," said Ella. "Take a look at the lake."

"I'll stay here," said Brad.

"No. We need your cheerful company."

The sun came up fast, blood-red. Just as quickly it mellowed to a pallid disk. They were a strange troupe, filing down the hill of the country lane without speaking. Honora walked on a few yards in front. Brad straggled behind. Ella and Lee wanted to grip hands but were for some reason impelled against it. It was no short distance to the lake, and in the chill, damp air of the early morning they completed the hike in silence.

When they got there, the lake was dead.

Or if not completely dead, it was locked in a state of suspended, strangled ugliness. The breath of spring, which abounded in everything else, had passed it by. A yellow, oily foam like detergent had collected in raked scum patterns on the surface of the water. It clung to dead branches and Coke cans and other debris at the lake's edge. The towering oak had failed to come into leaf and the rough bark was stripping itself on the side leaning over the water. The willow that had once dipped into the lake would never recover; it had withered into dry twigs and run the color of rust. The colonies of birds and insects that should have regenerated had either died with the lake or had migrated, never to return.

"Where did all this pollution come from?" said Brad. He sounded as if he took it personally.

Ella found some kind of an answer pinned to a tree. It was a notice of a public meeting, placed there by a Conservationist group.

POLLUTION

If you are disturbed by the pollution of this and other
areas of local beauty by the illegal dumping of
chemical wastes, please attend the public inquiry to be
held in Penmarthern Town Hall. Representatives of
the Lytex chemicals company will be in attendance.

The notice was already out of date: the meeting had gone by
two days earlier.

"Lytex?" said Lee, puzzling over the notice. "Sounds familiar."

"Forget it," said Brad.

Honora stood at the very edge of the lake. "It's poisoned," she
said, gazing into its depths. Then her face set in that same expression Ella had identified earlier. She swayed slightly on the bank
above the polluted water, as if played on some invisible cord, with
some still, small part of herself unwinding into the lake. Ella saw it
again. Honora looked pale, beautiful and unearthly, but anaemic, as
if her life-blood was leaking away. This time it was Brad who made
a move to save her, but Ella stopped him with a gesture. Then she
stepped forward, put an arm around the other woman and turned
her away from the water.

"I'm losing myself," said Honora.

"It's all right. I'll watch over you."

Lee fingered the diseased bark of the tall oak. Ella peered from
the bank as the iridescent scales of a detergent slick writhed slowly on
the water. Even amid the corruption and pollution she could see the
shining scales of a dragon, or a winged serpent, or a beautiful, silver-
armored company with banners fluttering below the surface of the
water. It was difficult to look away. "Let's get out of here," she said.

She led them from the lake over to the woods, where afternoons
had been spent strolling in Burns's company, when they were wide
eyed and receptive to his sharp definitions of life and to his quiet
revelations. Even in waking time on those afternoons, Burns had

made the woods a place of jewelled cobwebs, a place inhabited by satyrs and dryads. Now they were wandering without purpose through the moldering scrub of a thin damp copse.

Ella was circumspect as they walked, constantly glancing around her as though she expected to discover something or to encounter someone. If the others noticed, they made no comment.

They took the path back to the house, Honora still in advance and decisively separated from Brad by the other two. Occasionally they changed positions. Ella was anxious about leaving Honora alone with her thoughts, where she was like a weak swimmer at risk from strong currents. She sent Lee up to talk with Honora; Ella dropped back to talk with Brad; then Lee talked to Brad and Ella with Honora; but Honora and Brad never talked. And all of this was conducted against the rumbling, prophetic thunder of what the night held. On this night, they must sleep and dream.

Brad hung his cropped head, eyes fixed on the narrow path before him as Ella walked at his side. "Why are we doing this?"

"To make a connection," said Ella, glancing hopefully about her.

"I've made a connection. Can I be excused now?"

Ella took his arm. She was softening to his helplessness.

"Do you really not remember, Ella?"

"Remember what?"

"That time. Of dreaming. Just the once."

"Don't start that again."

"It's important to me."

"I'm sure it is."

"There's a reason why," he said softly, even shyly. "You say that it didn't happen—"

"Which it didn't."

"So I can't change that; it's what you remember, and anyway it was only on dreamside, but Ella it was *lucid*, there was no mistake, we all of us know the difference between those dreams and ordinary dreams, but you and I were there, alone and it was special, happy, for both of us, and for me it was the only time it ever happened . . ."

"What?" cried Ella.

"I don't mean the only time it ever happened, I mean the only time it happened—and I'm talking about waking time as well—that was real or good."

There was a frightening urgency about what Brad was saying. Ella closed her eyes. She wondered whether she could in fact recall such a situation with Brad, and conceded that underneath their old antagonism something sexual might have been afoot. Was there a fragment of a dream she had wiped out, repressed completely? Ella knew how easy it was to erase lucid dream experiences. She forced the thought back.

Up ahead, Lee and Honora were engaging in another version of that same conversation.

"What's the purpose of this?" Honora asked.

Lee didn't know, except that Ella wanted it. Sometimes he thought that Ella was just too complicated for him. He didn't understand half of the things she said and did, but he always went along with them. She acted and he reacted. She was quicksilver, he was lead. He had allowed himself to live too vaguely, and consequently she had led him since day one, often into places where he didn't want to be, and he was still following her now. How strongly Honora contrasted with Ella. She looked pale and vulnerable, but lovely in her simple woollen dress and plaited hair.

"Do you still think it could have been us?" said Lee.

"No point thinking of it now."

"No."

But after a pause she admitted, "I've always hung on to secret thoughts about you. Not love, or maybe not, at least let's not call it that. And I think you knew all about it."

"Never," said Lee. He kissed her lightly. This time there were no visions of serpents. Only a fresh smell like clear rainwater, and the diffuse sunlight a-play in her copper hair.

Ella watched from a short distance behind.

Late in the walk, Brad dropped behind Lee and Ella to talk to Honora. She shivered as he approached.

"I wanted to speak to you, Honora."

"What in hell would I have to say to you?"

"What about some recognition? What about sorry?"

"Sorry? You think I should apologize to you? You're demented as well as a drunkard."

"All of the times I tried to reach you; to help you. You never once bothered to answer. Time after time, over the years. Not once. Not a single word. Do those two know that? Not a bit of it. They're much happier to see me as the villain. It's all poor bloody Honora."

"I owe you nothing at all; nothing."

"You're wrong, Honora. You owe me the recognition. Did you tell them I was with you when it happened? Did you tell them I was there, and that I held your hand and warmed you, and cleaned you and delivered the baby on dreamside for you—did you tell them that? Did you tell them?"

She stopped and and turned to face him. "It was a different dream. You were never there. It could never have been the same dream."

"It was the same dream. I *was* there. You could never have done it alone, you would have died. That's why you ignored all my letters. You've just changed the dream. You've edited it, blocked me out, that's all. You all block me out!"

"It's not possible."

"It's the truth. My dream and your dream were the same dream."

"Why in God's name did you want to go stirring it all up, waking us all again? It was all dead and buried! Why couldn't you just leave us all in peace? It was all in the past until you brought it on us again. You brought it all back. They thought it was me, all of this time they thought that it was me doing it out of guilt. But I knew it was your doing. I just hoped it wasn't."

"You don't understand, I couldn't leave it. There was something belonging to us there which had to be settled, had to be put right. I didn't choose it; I was taken there and shown it time and time again. I couldn't hold it off."

"Like you can't hold off a drink you mean?"

"Maybe. I don't know. But I didn't intend to drag everyone else back in."

"You didn't 'intend'."

"Listen to me, Honora, I'm trying to make amends." He took hold of her arm. "It doesn't make any difference what you say, I've run out of fight."

"Brad Cousins, I don't care if you run out of breath."

Brad dropped her arm, and walked off in the opposite direction.

They had almost reached the house when Ella and Lee realized that Brad had disappeared.

"Where is he?"

"Gone."

"But is he coming back?"

"I don't know," said Honora.

She thought not.

ELEVEN

Lose your dreams and you might lose your mind
—Mick Jagger

With Brad gone, Ella thought that her plan had collapsed. But Lee found him back at the house a couple of hours later. He turned up in the old shed at the bottom of the garden, where the rowing boat had originally been stored.

When Lee had first tried the door he'd found it unlocked, but something barred his way in. Hammering the door open a few inches, forcing enough space for him to put his head around, he saw a faded relic of their summer idyll: the rowing boat, its paint cracked and peeling. It was carrying a strange load: Brad Cousins, sleeping heavily, legs draped across the stern. He was cradling an empty bottle of good malt whiskey. A second bottle lay discarded on the floor. Broken rays of sunlight stroked his bloated cheek.

"Hey Captain!" Lee shouted, relieved to have found him in any condition. Brad only slept on. Lee called again. There was no movement, and he returned to the house.

"Sleeping beauty just turned up. We'd better organize some coffee."

"Black?"

"Black as the pit."

Lee felt heartened; Ella's plan might still be salvaged. He

returned to the shed with a chipped mug of sweet, steaming black coffee. Squeezing into the shed, he set the coffee down on the workbench and tried to wake Brad gently.

First he tried shaking him by the arm. Then he patted his cheeks. Even bellowing loudly in his ear produced no result. His pats turned to hard slaps, but Brad slept on. It was only as a mischievous last resort that he considered a bucket of icy water.

With protracted ceremony, Lee filled the bucket. Ella and Honora followed behind him to enjoy the show, giggling through the shed window as he raised it aloft. They watched Brad get a thorough dousing. But where he was expected to scramble awake, puffing and groping blindly, he slept on. For the first time it occurred to Lee that getting him to wake up might be beyond their ability.

Maneuvering Brad's sleeping body out of the shed was a difficult task. The shed doors were blocked by the boat, and they were unable to move it because of Brad's considerable weight. Getting Brad out of the boat was no simpler. There was precious little room to stand alongside, let alone hoist Brad out, and he was a dead weight. Finally Lee managed to drag his lifeless, soaking body clear, as Ella manipulated the boat free of the doors, and eventually, sweating and swearing, Lee laid Brad down on the damp grass outside the shed. Ella kneeled beside him. His face felt dry and was bruised and bloated. There was a bubble of vomit at the corner of his lips.

"His hands are freezing, and his breathing is very shallow. We'd better get him to a hospital."

"I'll take him," said Lee. "Bring a blanket and help me get him to the car."

It was late afternoon when Lee returned. "Alcohol poisoning. He's in a coma."

"This much we already know," Ella said sharply.

"It's all they could say. He's comatose."

"When will he not be comatose?"

"They pumped his stomach. He didn't revive. The doctor said he could come out of it in five minutes. But it could be weeks, months, years. They've got him all wired up. There was no point in me hanging around drinking coffee from a plastic cup. So I left. Wasn't that the best thing to do?"

"And they said that it was the booze for sure?"

"They said so. But they were surprised it was such a heavy coma. They asked me a lot of questions about his lifestyle, which I couldn't answer. We just have to wait until he comes out of it. They said it's a condition beyond . . ."

"Beyond the help of medical science." Honora supplied the phrase.

"Something like that."

"Where does that leave us?" said Ella.

"One down, three to go?" said Honora.

The remark was left unanswered.

Evening drew in, and little was said. The silences prickled against the walls and crawled into every crevice and corner of the house. Every sound or movement was an affront. Mattresses had been dragged downstairs and covered with bedding so that later they could sleep side by side in the living room. This arrangement was made by tacit consent, an indication not of their closeness but of their fear of the night ahead.

Ella was the most worried. This strange turn in events had deflated her plans. She had staked everything on the idea of them taking the dreamside walk. She looked defeated.

Candle flames flickered from the mantelpiece, imparting shadows and inflaming imaginations that needed dampening. Outside a gate banged. Then it banged again and again in a mischievous wind, until Lee went out to fasten it.

It was a clear night. A moon was up, a slender crescent amid a scattering of bright stars, like the sable flag of a strange country. Lee looked into the sky for omens, portents. It was a moon for dreamers, cutting through the night sky and bearing strange cargo.

A scattering of lights burned in the distant village. They seemed a long way off, and something was stirring out there in the dark. Something was in this new wind, something which would never be seen nor smelled nor tasted, but which Lee sensed, fattening all around them.

"When will you leave us alone?" he said.

He was exhausted. Lack of sleep hung from him like chains, and played tricks with his eyes. As he looked up, everything took on a brilliant hallucinatory property. The moon hovered over him, bright, massive, leaking light everywhere, silver moonstain running from it like hot wax from a candle. The wind whipped up high, and he had a notion that he could see it, etched in rich, dark colors against the night sky. He could see its spiralling contours, its playful currents and its fan-shaped terraces. Then he shivered and went back inside.

TWELVE

Thy thoughts have created a creature in thee; and he
whose intense thinking thus makes him a
Prometheus; a vulture feeds upon that heart for ever
—Herman Melville

The house was like a camp under siege, with the enemy tents of ghost armies pitched in the garden outside. Ella tried to kindle a fire in the hearth, a brave attempt to smuggle some cheer into the room. The fire took at the third effort, smoky flames licking without relish at a damp log dropped on Ella's criss-cross of smoldering twigs. The key of a sardine can broke and Lee cut himself trying to extract the contents. They consumed a dismal meal in silence.

Lee suggested that someone should telephone the hospital ward, to get a report on Brad's condition. Since no telephone had been installed in the house, this involved a short drive to the nearby village. This small task took on the prospect of a minatory expedition with all attendant dangers. Lee's recent tangle with telephones was a strong disincentive. He seemed to think that Ella should be the one to go, and said so. But Ella had been looking for an opportunity to speak privately with Lee. She needed some minutes alone with him, even though she was disinclined to leave Honora, whose capacity to remain in complete possession of herself seemed to be deteriorating fast.

"Look at her!" she said. She'd addressed Honora twice, without getting any response. Honora was staring into the fire with an expressionless, unfocused gaze. Her eyes lacked luster, seemingly dried out by the smoke. She was away. "You can see her uncoiling. It's almost *physical!*"

Ella took Honora's hand and broke the enchantment.

"Come away from the fire."

"It happened again? I'm like smoke. I'm coming apart."

"We're going to phone. Come with us."

"I'd rather not go out there."

"It would be better if you came."

"Don't make me go out there, Ella."

Ella hesitated. "We'll be ten minutes at the most."

Ella made the call, with Lee hovering in the background. Brad's condition was unimproved. He was still in a critical state. Ella sighed and replaced the receiver. She told Lee what she had heard and they agreed to telephone again in the morning. Before they climbed back into the car, Ella took Lee by the sleeve.

"She's right isn't she? What she said about it today. She just knows it."

Lee nodded. "Honora is all intuition. She's the most susceptible."

"Meaning what?"

"Meaning she knows how it will be. The danger of being overwhelmed. Of dreaming and never finding our way back. Of being stitched into the fabric of dreaming, frozen in perpetual dreamside."

"It's the worst scenario. The worst nightmare."

"It's what we face now."

"I just didn't want to admit it. To myself."

Lee looked at her. Ella's eyes were as honest as the sky. Where did she get her courage from? He grabbed her cold white hand and kissed it. "Like you said, it's the worst nightmare of all. Perhaps one of us will have to stay awake, while the others dream. Perhaps that's the only way."

"Short straws? Or volunteers?" Ella shook her head. "It won't work. We all have to be there on dreamside. We're all implicated."

"If only we had someone on the outside of our dreaming, some-one to anchor us. If Burns was here, what would he tell us? What clue would he give us?"

Ella recalled her motorway encounter with the professor—if indeed it was the professor—and saw him vividly: agitated, cryptic, wringing his hands; saying nothing she could understand.

"Listen to this. I had an encounter on the motorway. I have to tell you about it, only there's an uncertainty. I met the professor: that is, I met him—or he came to me—but I don't know if it was really him. Maybe it was someone else. I know I'm sounding confused and maybe I'm making a mistake here . . . Only it *was* the professor who came to me in the car, after a nasty experience I had. I felt sure he—she, it—was trying to help us."

"What did he say?"

"Nothing we can use. Something about undoing what was done. He got very agitated."

"But that's all that was said?"

" 'Undo what was done.' "

"Not exactly a lifeline, is it?"

"Wherever it came from, I looked back and saw not Burns, but . . . Oh, why are we afraid to name it? I saw not the professor, but the Other."

"But it still doesn't help."

"No."

"We need a thread. Something to take into the labyrinth which will lead us out again. It's got to be you, Ella. You're the seer out of all of us, you're the one. Can't you weave us a golden thread?"

"Made out of what? You overestimate me Lee, you always did. Maybe Honora will be the one who finds the way. Come on, let's go."

———

At that moment Honora was in need of a golden thread of her own.

The moment that the door had closed after them, Honora regretted her decision to wait behind. The damp air inside the house chilled her, and she was terrified of what might be stalking them outside. Her nerves shivered like ice in a cracked glass.

The house felt strangely hollow, like a burial chamber. She got up and moved around the room, arms folded defensively, self-consciously avoiding the seductive powers of the fire and the candle flame. The wind got up again outside, moaning in the tall trees and swinging the gate back and forth.

From the open doorway she could see the gate swaying slowly in the shadows. Then it slapped hard against the gatepost, and swung open again. It was possible to make out the silhouette of a small figure crouched over the gate. It was no more than a shadow, bobbing backwards and out of view as the gate swayed open.

"Who's there?" said Honora. She hesitated on the doorstep, and then tentatively touched her foot on the path. There was the figure again, like a small, cowled thing. The gate stopped moving and the silhouette ducked behind it. Honora moved slowly down the path, one hand outstretched towards the gate. It banged violently shut.

Honora recovered. It was only the wind, the figure just a waving rhododendron bush behind the gate. With relief she secured the stiff latch and slid home the rusting bolt.

But back indoors she heard a scratching at the window pane. Someone was at the window. She moved slowly towards it.

It was the wind, riffling the straggling ornamental bushes, pressing their branches against the glass. Then there was a sighing in the garden—the wind in the ragged strips of broken fencing. A scuffling behind the house—only the wind, chasing a scrap of torn newsprint. The sound of banging at the front of the house. The wind again, slapping the gate back and forth. The gate which, only a moment earlier, Honora herself had carefully secured.

She looked out of the window, through her own reflection. The gate had somehow freed itself. It swung gently back and forth. An arched silhouette rode it, like a child on a wooden horse—surely only the curved back of the rhododendron, a trick of the shadows. Honora let the curtain fall and sat down before the fire.

The sound of scratching on the window returned. It was a sound like fingernails drawn down the pane of glass. She ignored it. It persisted. It was followed by a tapping, a slow, regular beating. Then a sound like that of a child breathing hard, a child misting up the glass with her mouth. Small, scuffling feet darted from front to back of the house. Honora pressed her hands to her ears.

The scratching and tapping on the window moved to the back of the house. Honora looked up. Now she saw the sickly, whey-colored face, mouthing at the glass, darting from one window pane to the other and tapping, almost playfully.

"No," moaned Honora covering her ears again, "no no *no*."

Then it stopped, and the figure went away. All Honora could hear now was the throaty rasp of her own breathing. She looked around her, wildly. There was nothing. She busied herself, becoming frantically methodical. She put another log on the fire, reeled to the kitchen, watched a kettle boil, brewed coffee and tried to talk herself into a state of calm.

She returned to the fireside, hugging her coffee to her like a shield. She counted off the seconds, as if each one were a sword-blow parried with diminishing strength. Slowly she became aware of a flicker at the edge of her vision, a dull phosphorescence: something had come into the room.

It filled the room and infected it with cold. Its presence was *strong*. Like tart moonlight, like acid frost, like sour, congealed breath. It was the color and taste and odor of neglect and decay masquerading as a human child. Honora's coffee slipped to the floor, a dark stain expanding in four directions.

Sitting in the chair opposite, the girl didn't speak. Her head was tilted to one side like a marionette. Her sheenless eyes were fixed on Honora. She was only too human, a waif in a sad cut-down dress. Her jaw was slack and her hair unkempt, not lovable, no, but infinitely pitiable. Her sand-colored eyes, the eyes of a dead seal, were fixed on Honora but looking through and past her, as if waiting for the answer to some question posed long ago, patiently but insistently waiting for the answer which never comes.

Honora was paralysed, like the very first dreamside paralysis. Her words choked. "When will you be done with us?"

The fixed expression on the girl's face slowly changed, twisting into a sneer. She stood up and moved towards the fire. Honora felt a wave of cold. There was the same phosphorescent halo about her, the glow of moon on water. It pulsed briefly before fading, and with the pulsing the girl diminished in size and substance, transforming at last into a small, hard lozenge of blue flame which arced like a tiny meteor, dropping into the fire.

Honora's eyes followed it into the heart of the fire. She had no will to resist, to look away. Even knowing the danger, and remembering Ella's warnings, that single conjured spark had been enough to draw her back. The fire held her, trancelike, and was drawing her in. She was a single thread; the fabric of her being was a many-textured, spectrum-colored tapestry, unravelling a fiber at a time, unwinding on to a vast spool held by hands within the fire, one fine strand carefully wound in after another. As if that is where it starts, at the eyes, where the threads of the soul hang in their slackest stitch; stitches which can be hooked free of weft and warp, and pulled through, drawn out, spooled in. She was lost to it. She was coming apart.

She knew the danger. The idea of resistance fashioned itself into a sword in her mind, a bright-edged sword, a way out. But the sword itself became smoke; and the thing she would slash free of became smoke. The effort to resist required too much, too mighty a cut, too great a mental stroke. Her mind was coming apart.

Honora belonged to the fire. She was enslaved by the ritual dance of the aromatic flame. Fire, first and most martial of all elements, the hierarchical prince. She saw in the fire the tapered banners of his glorious armies, the swallowtail pennants a-flutter, flags of crimson, ochre, sapphire, armies spilling into valleys and camped along the plains. They pinioned her and they held her. The flame engaged with her. She was fire. She was smoke. She was coming apart, like smoke.

"Burning! What's burning?" Lee and Ella stood over her, shaking her.

"Honora!" They were calling her as if from a great distance.

Lee dragged her to her feet, shaking her violently, stripping off her outer clothes. Slowly she became aware of a thick, acrid smell, and realized that the room was fogged with dense, grey smoke.

"Are you burned? Honora, are you burned?" Lee was frantically stroking her arms.

"No."

Miraculously she wasn't. At her feet she saw, still smoldering but not even charred, the skirt and pullover which Lee had torn from her. Wisps of smoke writhed from the clothes. Ella was running around opening windows.

"What happened?" Honora was still dazed.

Lee and Ella just looked at each other. Ella folded Honora in her arms as the other woman wept.

"It has to be tonight," said Ella. "It has to be tonight."

THIRTEEN

If the doors of perception were cleansed everything
would appear as it is, infinite
—William Blake

Surely tonight sleep will come. But sleep is choosy these days about the company she keeps. And those who may have been caught in the past with a stolen fistful of her soft plumage can't complain if now she makes them wait for favors. So the three lie on their mattresses in the dark, and wait.

Lee shifts in a half-sleep, perspiring heavily, unable to find the elusive groove. Honora doses herself with another of her pills, frets, hugs her knees, stifling her own whimpers. But long after sleep has finally taken them, Ella lies awake. She curls stiffly in the darkness, disturbed by a stroboscopic flickering behind her closed eyes. Responsibility weighs on her. She feels accountable for them all, a burden which comes from being the strongest of the four dreamers. She suspects that in the end they might stand or fall by her efforts alone.

"Make us a thread," Lee had pleaded. "A golden thread. Something to take in with us that might lead us out."

She dredges the limits of her memory. There had to be something from which she could create Lee's golden thread. A special kind of thread. A thread which could span from outer world to inner mind like a glittering bridge, as light and fluid as dream itself.

She swoops back over her encounter on the motorway. There is only a vague conversation, leaving here with nothing more than instructions to *undo what was done*.

It's hopeless. There's nothing there. Nothing.

Night marches on, and sleep eludes her. Occasionally, one of the others stirs under their blankets. Ella looks up briefly and sinks back on to her own bed of nails.

She can see Burns with perfect clarity, offering her his unhelpful advice and wringing his hands in anguish. In her feverish vision he grows more and more impatient, more anguished, twisting his arthritic fingers together: *Can't you see, Ella, it's you, it's you, I can't do it for you, can't you see that it's not in my—*

HANDS.

Ella sits bolt upright.

There's a moment of panic. She's terrified that the idea which just came to her might slip away, snuff out like a candle flame. She's trying to hold on to something. Hold the idea there, gently, carefully; she looks at the other two sleepers for help. They don't stir. She leans back on the pillow.

Yes Ella, it's in your hands.

That's what Burns was trying to tell you all the time.

The dream exercise comes back to her. The hand manipulation game. It's a fragment of childhood, something taken from the bottomless toy chest of the mind at play. The dream exercise. The one they had created between them. The one that had formed the original bridge, the bridge between early lucid dreaming and true dreamside control.

That's how it was, how it *always* was. Dreaming from the head through the hands, miraculously working to transform the external world . . . Slow down! thinks Ella. *Slow down!* Her mind is struggling against something which wants her to deviate from the track, stray off course, lose her fix.

Undo what was done, Burns's phantom had said to her. But

what was done? And *how* was it done? Let's take it slow. Very slow. And with all the power of childlike lucidity. For this is how it was.

Here is the church.

She sees two women talking in the ruins of a bombed-out cathedral. They are disputing, or perhaps testing out, the reality of a dreamside birth. A child, a thing—no, a child—was conceived and delivered on dreamside. The church, that's the womb, the woman, thinks Ella, her eyes raking the darkened ceiling. And the tower, the steeple tall and erect, that's the man. It's so clear. *Here is the church, here is the steeple*. A woman and a man.

Open the door. Yes, that's lovemaking all right. Open the door, call it by another name, sex, or here a violation where love is absent, but open the door. *And here are the people*. There it is, the birth, the propagation of the people, born to start the cycle of life all over again.

But where does all this lead? It's just a child's game, isn't it? A shadow play, a sleight of hand. A little story with a twist and nothing else. Or is there more? Another strand to the thread? Like the words changing in the books on dreamside, can the thread change to give more?

Try again.

Here is the church. Why yes, that's our belief, our faith in brave dreaming. *Here is the steeple*. There is our aspiration, the wish to dream, the soaring desire to make it happen. *Open the door*, the door of sleep, the door to the place of dreaming. *And here are the people*. Who are the people? We are the people. Born out of faith and desire, we are the dreamers, the dreamers of dreams.

It's easy. The golden thread has as many strands as you care to make, as many as there are interpretations. Ella is feverish. She can see a golden thread spinning out to a point beyond her vision. Sparks of pure golden light shimmer and dart from it as it spins in rapid style from the turning of her mind. This is the thread they will transport to dreamside, as light and as fluid as dream itself. But there is one essential strand to the thread which must be strong enough to lead them out again afterwards.

She knows she's on to something. If it can be found, it will be found here. Only now tiredness closes her in. It folds down on her. She feels the edges of consciousness retreat like the outposts of an empire. Now she has to fight sleep.

Perhaps it's just a question of viewing the thread in reverse. Like examining the stitching on the reverse side of an embroidery. The question is, does the key fit the lock from both sides of the door? And can the thread pay out a third time?

Church. And if the church was our faith in dreaming, then mistrust must be its opposite. What if that mistrust itself has become the instrument of oppression? A church which has become a prison, wasn't that the measure of their dreaming now?

Steeple. We made a Babel of vanity and an arrogance out of out desire to dream, to climb as high as God. Indifference is the opposite of desire, and the worst crime of all. And we fell asleep. We made a crisis of faith out of mistrust and indifference. Will we ever find our way back?

Door. How do we open the doorway back? How do we recover our faith and our desire?

But Ella can go no further. She is too drained to think it through; too tired to spin the thread any longer; too exhausted to finish weaving the strand. The last flickering candle has burned down to a gob of wax. Her mind closes down like a square of paper neatly folded in on itself, and then once again, and then again.

FOURTEEN

"If that there King was to wake,"
added Tweedledum, "you'd go out—bang!—
just like a candle!"
—Lewis Carroll

Ella only knew that sleep had finally taken her when she became aware she was on *dreamside*. Lee was standing close by. He was look- ing at her strangely.—I've been waiting—he thoughtspoke.— You're here. It feels cold—

He touched her, and brought her to him. In the embrace they rediscovered that shivering intensity, the tremulousness beneath the surface of things, but with something else, something extra.

A colorless, tasteless, odorless sense, oppressive and insistent. It grabbed like a hand inside the stomach, itching at the very mem- brane of dreamside. It was the claw of a dread anxiety. Something predatory hung watchful on the air.

—Is anyone else here?—Before Ella had even completed the thought, she saw Honora standing under the oak, looking out over the frozen snow-covered lake. She seemed carved from ivory. The scene was encompassed in still mists.

Everywhere was ice; mist-bound and ice-locked. Dreamside was precisely as Honora knew it, and exactly as Ella and Lee had glimpsed it on their single fleeting return visit. It was a mockery of the place it had once been, and a snowbound shadow of the polluted lake as it was now.

They waited, scraping their boots on the frozen grass at their feet. Even those small movements seemed ready to burst the dream as they waited for the one who was missing.

—Must we have him here Ella?—

—We all have to be present—Ella was firm, authoritative. Perhaps she knew more than she was saying. She seemed certain in the knowledge that the fourth member of the group would appear. They waited; and they waited.

Brad came from nowhere. He came wide-eyed, and in a dangerously befuddled state. He stopped short of them, like a nervous animal, staring at the ground. They all watched him, but were afraid of him. They didn't dare to speak to him, and even sought to disguise their thoughts. They stood rigidly, like figurines carved from a single piece of horn.

Brad seemed confused, lost. He looked from one to the other as if he was about to speak. Then he looked wildly over his shoulder. He moved closer to Ella, mouthing words that failed to come. Then:—Help me—

—What is it Brad?—

—Can't awaken. Can't wake up. Help me Ella!—

Brad was stricken with panic. His eyes were all black pupil and they leaked frosty tears. He stood close enough for Ella to feel his cold breath on her face. She put out a hand to touch him and was shocked to find him stiff with frost. He snatched at her hand and gripped it fiercely. The cold from his fingers burned, and her skin seemed to sear and stick fast to his. Their eyes locked as he dared her to snatch her hand away.

At last he relaxed his hold. Ella felt a blistering pain as she withdrew her hand: she felt a fine layer of skin ripping from the back of her wrist where he had gripped her.

—The dream won't break Ella, the dream won't break—

—We're all here Brad. We're not going to desert you—

—You can't do anything. The dream won't break. I'm tired from staying awake. So tired. And we have to stay awake. Awake. They're waiting for me to sleep. The ice. The frost. The cold. They wait for you to sleep. And then they take you—

Ella saw it clearly. She didn't need to be reminded of the predatory nature of the elementals. She could recall their attacks with vivid horror. How they waited for the moment before sleep within the wheel of the dream. How they silently infiltrated invisible tendrils into the blood and fiber and flesh of your dreaming body. Transforming you, until you were lost to earth or water or fire or ice. But now she saw for the first time that the elementals were not a group of entities at all, not a colony of predatory beings. They were all a single expression of the same force, the life-creating and life-devouring, birth-giving and soul-sucking power of dreamside.

And now the toughened membrane of the dream wouldn't break. Brad had been trapped, to walk in terror of the sleep within sleep, of being imprisoned for ever in the ice-sleep. No one could stay awake indefinitely, here as within the waking world. Brad was merely postponing the inevitable. Even now the frost was squeezing him, congealing his blood. This was the fate of those who stayed too long on dreamside.

—This is how it will be for all of us—It was Honora. She seemed strangely resigned.—This is how it will be—

—None of us will wake! There is no waking!—A tear welled at the corner of Brad's eye. In a moment his anguish gave way to laughter, the laughter of a maniac, echoing eerily across the mist-shrouded lake, jagged laughter which ricocheted back at them, and sliced through the air. Ella shot a panicked look at Lee.

But Lee was pointing at something on the edge of the lake. The other three turned, their eyes following the direction of his finger. Brad's laughter stopped.

—It's her—He swayed unsteadily.

—I knew it—Ella breathed.

—She's the one!—Brad shouted.—She's the one who is keeping me here. She's the one who will keep us all here!—

But they already knew. She stood twenty feet away from them, in an ill-cut dress, her skin the color of milk and her eyes like black holes. Only here she looked stronger, stronger than them. They all knew her, and they were all afraid of her. They gazed at her stupidly. Her eyes blazed back at them. An aching loneliness blew from her like an icy wind.

—Speak to us—Honora approached timidly.—Please speak to us—

But the girl tossed her hair and set foot on the frozen lake, glancing over her shoulder as if daring them to follow. Honora took a few steps towards her.

—Honora, don't!—It was Lee calling her back.

—Wait! Wait and watch!—This time it was Ella, unsure whether to trust the girl; unsure whether their roadside encounter had been a snare set with treacherous clues.

The girl paced farther out on to the ice. Honora hesitated at the edge of the frozen water.

—Don't go!—Lee commanded.

—It's a trap! She wants you to go out on the ice!—Brad was hysterical.—It's a trick! You mustn't trust her! Don't trust her! I know who she is!—

The girl stopped and turned to them, as if she was waiting. She mouthed something incomprehensible. As she saw Honora set a tentative foot on to the ice, she turned and proceeded out into the middle of the lake. Honora looked back at Ella, who nodded almost imperceptibly. She began to walk across the ice. Ella left the others and followed her.

Lee's protests strangled in his throat. He found himself following the two women out on to the lake, with Brad staying close behind him. It was if the four of them were roped together. When the girl came to a halt, they all stopped short.

She looked back at them again. Then she scuffed at the ice with the edge of her shoe. She scraped away a layer of snow and scratched at the ice, never averting her gaze from them. She looked away only to stoop and to rub at the tiny clearing she had scratched in the snow. Then she moved away from the clearing she had made and stood at a distance.

Honora was the first to approach. She looked through the cleared patch to the gluey grey formations of ice beneath. What did it mean? Honora and Ella looked to the girl for an answer, but she had turned defiantly towards the shore.

Brad had reached the cleared space and was on his knees, rubbing at the surface of the ice with an outstretched hand and peering at the geometric shapes below.

—There's something there—he said.

The others turned slowly.

—There's something there. I can see it. Under the ice—

—What? What is it?—Lee kneeled beside him.

—It's under the ice. It's trying to get out—

—What can you see there?—

—It's trying to get out! IT WANTS TO GET OUT FROM UNDER THE ICE!—

—Tell us what you see!—Ella commanded.

But Brad was half-crazed. He seemed to detect a new movement.—It's moving! It's waving! Look! It's trying to get out of there! It wants to get out!—

Suddenly his body went rigid, his breath coming in short gulps.

Lee bundled him aside and began pawing at the ice himself, clearing away the snow on the surface. In mounting horror he saw what Brad had seen. It was an image of Brad beneath the ice, hoary and encrusted, bruised and blackened and floating like a corpse— but it wasn't dead. It was waving rigidly, pressing against the under-surface, mouthing silent words that distorted the face, trying to find a way out.

The image of Brad was not alone. Three other figures floated there. Images of Lee, Ella and Honora, all pressing against the ice and mouthing unheard cries. They were all prisoners.

Now they all saw it. They were hypnotized by the revelation. They were fixed, locked into the images of themselves, gazing down in horror at this shivering incarnation of their enjoined destinies. They felt the elemental cold slowly beginning to transfer itself to them, to still the flow of their blood.

—We're trapped—whispered Honora.—It's the dream within the dream—

Lee looked to Ella, but her eyes were on the little girl. The girl was kneeling on the frozen lake, hands clasped in anguish beneath her chin like someone at prayer, eyes streaming with tears as she sobbed uncontrollably. Ella was mesmerized. Lee saw in Ella's eyes a glitter, like sunlight on frost, of the mad priestess. He realized with shock and admiration that she was about to take charge. Her confidence fluttered around her like a protective cloak.

—Keep moving! Don't stand still! We have to undo what was done!—Ella's words eclipsed everything. She had remembered the golden thread she had been spinning before falling asleep. It came out like a formula, like a spell.

—Church and steeple! Door and people!—She was yelling at them, without shifting her eyes from the kneeling, weeping girl.— Faith and desire! We have to end our mistrust! No more indifference! Honora, take your curse from Brad's head! Do it *now!*—

—How can I?—

—Just lift it! Lift the curse!—

—But it's only words! Words are not real things!—

—Just! Lift! It!—

—I unmake it I unmake it I unmake it!—Honora was screaming. She was hysterical. She wanted to run to the girl but Ella held her back.

—Open the door! We must open the door! Can't you see it! Open the door and the people will escape! Here are the people! We are the people! Dream a hole in the ice!—

But Ella didn't wait for the others. She turned her gaze on the clearing of snow, at the figures floating beneath the ice. Remaining perfectly still she recalled all the forgotten powers of dreaming and focused them on the submerged figures. She was willing the ice to melt. Lee and Brad were activated by her raw energy. They followed her lead blindly, standing perfectly still, concentrating their minds, dreaming a hole in the frozen water. And slowly the ice began to melt.

None of them heard Honora moaning softly.—I've been in this dream before! You must stop! I've seen this!—

It was too late. Tiny hairline cracks suddenly began to appear in the ice, multiplying and discharging in all directions. There was a thudding sound from somewhere beneath them, like the banging together of great ice floes or the grinding of huge rocks.

—No! No!—

Now Lee saw what Honora was most afraid of. It was his turn to panic.—We have to get off the ice!—

—Not yet! Break open the ice! Dream open the door! Release the people! Here is your golden thread, Lee!—Ella still commanded the situation.

The lake answered. From deep, deep under the ice came a low, blasphemous groan. There was a series of dull, sonorous thuds like distant detonations, followed by a terrible tearing sound. The ice began to tremble.

—Wait! Wait!—

This time the sound of groaning and splitting sounded loudly in their ears and a violent tremor in the ice sent them rocking. Ella staggered backwards. The cracks in the ice expanded into jagged black forks, splitting off in all directions. Lee saw that Honora and Brad were paralyzed. They wanted to escape from the lake but were unable to tear themselves away. Ella was still locked into the consummation of the ritual she had initiated. He couldn't seem to make her hear him. She was entranced by the ugly, multiplying fractures in the ice. Lee shook her violently. She looked back at him as though he were someone from another world. It was like looking across time.

The ice was splitting everywhere. Ella came to her senses. She took hold of Honora. Lee propelled both of them towards the bank. They clung to each other, slipping and skidding as they tried to scramble off the ice. With the sound of ice splitting and splintering around them, Lee hoisted Brad off his knees; but in flailing and staggering wildly Brad brought them both down. Lee tried to struggle to his feet but Brad clung desperately to his legs. The two men slithered hopelessly.

Ella and Honora stood on the edge of the bank screaming at them. Brad groped blindly at Lee, dragging him back. At last they scrambled to the edge, where the two women pulled them to safety.

—The girl!— said Honora.—Where is the girl?—

No one answered. Behind them was a mass of deep interlacing cracks, darting across the lake like snakes' tongues and splitting still farther as they watched. Then the ice began to groan like a wounded primeval beast, folding against itself and crushing upwards, breaking up in huge slabs which collapsed in clouds of steam. Churning grey waters tossed in the air, waters that broiled and bubbled and released billowing jets of cloud.

A wind of hurricane strength blew up from nowhere, or from within the depths of the lake itself. It threatened to pick them up like straws. The willows screamed as the wind tore through their dead branches, and the old charred oak creaked and leaned with the wind. Ella stood behind its huge trunk, her hair whipping in her eyes as she called to the others, urging them to make a chain around the tree. But the wind stole the words off her mouth as she reached out for Lee and pulled him to her. Honora saw them, and with the hurricane shrieking and raging around her and the water boiling behind her, she took hold of Brad's outstretched arm and battled to reach Lee and Ella.

—Circle the tree! Circle the tree!—Ella was mouthing orders that none of the others could hear. The lake was now a boiling cauldron, releasing great geysers of water and steam thirty feet into the air. Huge waves radiated from the center, buffeted by the wind and crashing on the banks of the lake, hissing and sizzling as they fell on frozen earth. Lee guessed what Ella was trying to do. He threaded his way around the tree trunk, inching into the full force of the hurricane, pulling the chain of the others after him. Circling the tree, he was able to link arms with Honora, but the force of the wind pressed him flat against the blackened trunk like a pin on a magnet. On the other side, Ella linked arms with Brad.

The earth at their feet was scooped up in giant handfuls and flung around their heads and into the lake. The wind was digging them out. The ruined oak creaked and groaned and leaned. The angry wind clawed like a live thing at the ground, throwing up earth and exposing its roots. It seemed that even the tree might be dug out and dragged into the lake. The four clung grimly to each other's arms, faces pressed against the charred trunk. Ella thought that if only they were able to hold on they might have a chance.

But the hurricane shrieked and howled like a thing enraged, and Ella slipped and fell as the earth was dug out from under her feet. The wind ripped up clods of earth and loose soil, tossing it in the air and lashing it at their faces. The others held her up as she found new footing on the exposed roots. Then the roots themselves curled and bent in the wind as if twisted by a giant fist. They began to snap, were torn off and bulleted into the lake. The tree groaned and leaned farther with the wind. It was being dug out of the earth.

Then Lee felt Honora stiffen, and saw her mechanically turn her head towards the boiling lake. Her features reset themselves in that familiar gaze. Her face was ivory. He felt her loosen her grip, as if she wanted to be taken by the wind, as if her resistance was exhausted. He knew that she was going into the lake.

—No Honora! No!—The wind lifted the words from his lips.

Ella saw what was happening.—Stop her!—

—I can see her in the water! She wants me! I'm going to her!— Honora slipped Lee's arm. He lunged to pull her back, but she fell away easily.

—Hold her! Keep her there!—Ella called out to Brad, knowing that somewhere in the storm he too was holding Honora. Then she felt Lee stumble towards her and a sudden absence of pressure at her other hand.

Brad had slipped Ella's hold and had gone with Honora. Ella and Lee slithered to the base of the tree, clinging to its exposed roots. They saw Honora plunge into the raging water, crying out unintelligibly into the heart of the storm. It was Brad who plunged in after her and dragged her, kicking and thrashing and screaming, out onto the bank. Then he fell or dived back into the water. Fell or dived they would never know, but they saw him look back at them as he was dragged under. Lee grabbed Honora and brought her weeping to the tree, where the three of them clung like survivors of a shipwreck groping for a plank of driftwood.

As quickly as it had appeared, the wind dropped, and the waters on the lake calmed. Brad did not come up again. The three lay panting, exhausted on the bank of the lake. Already it was beginning to ice over. Then the dream broke.

EPILOGUE

*I do not know whether I was then a man dreaming
I was a butterfly, or whether I am now a butterfly
dreaming I am a man*
—Chuang Tzu, 3rd century BC

Ella checked her face in the hotel room mirror. After packing and clearing her room she decided to forgo breakfast and leave early. Carrying her split-leather holdall down the stairs, she crossed the polished parquet floor to the reception desk, where she learned that Lee had already taken care of the bill. She was grateful for that since money was going to be a problem for a while. Then she went outside and crossed the deserted hotel car park, unlocking the door of the Midget before swinging her bag on to the passenger seat.

The sun was well up in the sky. The morning was fresh but tranquil, and it promised to be a beautiful spring day. She readjusted the soft-top of the Midget to its down position, and the clip which Lee had repaired for her came apart in her hands. Since there was no one else around, Ella allowed herself another weep, last one before leaving.

"Come on, Innes, you'll see worse than this," she said into a crumpled tissue. But she was crying for a whole host of things. Ella had agreed to stay behind for a few days to tidy up the details. In the end, she had felt most responsible, particularly for Brad.

It was she, after all, who had raced down to Cornwall to bring him back. She had cooked up the whole plan; and it was she who had gone alone to the hospital that morning after the ultimate dream. When she had woken the morning after the storm on dreamside—incredibly only three days ago—she had not waited for the other two. She had got into her car and had driven to the hospital with a terrible foreknowledge. It echoed an earlier experience in her life. It had been a fine morning, like this one, of diffuse yellow sunshine and the grass wet with a heavy dew.

She had thought of the time she had washed him and shaved him and cut his hair and dressed him, ostensibly in preparation for meeting the others but really for their last walk on dreamside. There had seemed to be a tiny measure of hope, but that was then. Of course she wished she hadn't done any of it, wished she had left Brad to his moldering alcoholic decay in Elderwine Cottage. But she knew that bringing him back to face that final dreamside rendezvous was as unavoidable as daylight coming after dark. Or the reverse; Ella wasn't sure.

She tried hard to recall the thing which he had begged her to remember. It grieved her deeply that she hadn't been able to see how important it might have been to Brad if she had just been able to lie—if indeed lie it was. But no; surely that would have made the entire dreamside business nothing more than a conspiracy. A conspiracy of what would at worst be a nest of liars, and at best a coven of hysterics. Yet it had all happened. And whatever they were, she was not about to betray or deny a single moment of the reality of dreaming.

At the hospital they told her that Brad had died during the night, that he'd never come out of his coma. There was some bewilderment on their part, and talk of a postmortem. Ella had said "Thank you" to the doctor who had broken the news. It had been an odd thing to say. What Ella had meant was thank you for the clarity, thank you for the confirmation of what she already knew, thank you for the permission to grieve. When she had returned to the house, to tell Lee and Honora what they too had already guessed, that's when her tears had come.

After he had held her for a while, Lee had cleared the house. He had suggested they stay in the town while the formalities of Brad's death were taken care of. That night they had checked into a hotel, where Lee had booked three single rooms.

In the morning, when Lee found himself alone with Ella, he told her that he wanted to return to Northern Ireland with Honora. Ella was not at all surprised.

"Honora wants it; but she won't do it because she thinks you will feel betrayed. I know that's not so, and I think you would have been leaving me anyway."

"Tell her I understand."

"I love you, Ella, but I'm no match for you and I'll never be enough for you."

"I'm not sure I know what you mean by that."

"Yes, you do."

"Lee, will you do me a favor and leave today? I'll stay here for another night or so."

"I can't leave you with all of this."

"I would prefer it. Really I would."

Lee knew that Ella didn't say things for the sake of form. She wanted Honora and him to go, so they did. Before they left, Ella hugged Honora and kissed her and they made unkeepable promises about seeing each other again. Then she went to Lee.

"Ella . . ." he began.

But she stopped him. "Now you're going to kiss me, and then you're going to go," she said, as if she were directing an actor.

Lovers were easy to come by, thought Ella. They were as thick on the ground as used dreams. But a relationship that would stand the test was rare. So she and Lee parted for the second time, and she never let him know that he was right, that she would have been leaving him anyway.

On her way out of town, Ella drove up to the lake to take a final look. The sun was warm, and at the top of the hill overlooking the lake she stopped the car and climbed out to see what was happening. A small army of volunteer conservationists had already begun the task of cleaning the polluted water. They were busy dredging, draining and replanting. Ella felt heartened. She wanted to go over and wish them luck, but she felt shy about it. She knew they would do a fine job.